THE BOY WITH THE SUN IN HIS EYES

THE BOY WITH THE SUN IN HIS EYES

A novel by James Derek Dwyer

A Bangor Book

Copyright © 2005 by James Derek Dwyer

All rights reserved under International and
 Pan-American Copyright Conventions.

Published in the United States of America by Bangor Books of
Boston, Massachusetts.

Library of Congress Control Number: 2004195787

ISBN0976495104

For Todd Verow

The best thing about the funeral was Solange. It was like catching yourself from falling down a flight of stairs. I'd heard Kevin talk her up so much I could almost do whole monologues about her. I had all her films--*The Rabid Ghouls, War for Water, Rat Attack!* etc.--on snowy, tracking-impaired VHS tapes, but I never got around to meeting her until Kevin died. I mean, he was going to introduce us but he died this time around before he had a chance.

At first, before seeing the movies and a few handwritten letters from her, I had thought that he had made her up. He was always inventing little characters, giving them scandalous little lives and then talking about them as if they were real to people who didn't know any better. For the longest time during college our answering machine's outgoing message was this weird mini-one act play that he had the two of us do. I think it lost more of our would-be suitors than it was worth, but he loved the way people would assume we were more interesting than we actually were. He was more than willing to turn his life into fictional escapades. Problems only came later when he made them real escapades.

I thought Solange was one of his make-pretend people. She wasn't; she was their impetus. He said that she had opened his mind to a lot of things. And for Kevin to say that meant something; his mind was born wide open. He had a brain like a toy chest.

Then Kevin went and shot himself in the toy chest. He was already dying of AIDS-related lymphoma. He just didn't want to wait around, I guess. He'd never been tested for HIV and then one day woke up with a tumor. Well, he woke up with a lot of pain then he went to the doctor and he was told that he was dying.

The last time I saw him; he dragged his I.V. bag out to the curb and took a pack of cigarettes from his hospital nightie. He lit up and sucked down the smoke like it was a cure.

"The nurses made me feel kinda weird about smoking- but then one of them said 'hell if I was you- I'd be smoking too.'"

"Heartwarming nightingales of medicine."

"You believe in an afterlife, Johnny-John?"

This was one of Kevin's trick questions, made even dicier because he had so much more riding on it than I did at the moment. At least, at the moment.

"Yeah- it's ah," Fumble, fumble. "Only logical that something continues, because, you know, infinity is full of infinite possibilities."

He didn't like that answer. Little wannabe theorist that I am, but he knew that about me and took it for what it was worth. He frowned a bit and stared at the emergency room door. "I guess so." He didn't say that in a sad voice, more a kind of curious question voice- then he did the patented Kevin subject switch. "I want to use this chemo-being-bald-thing for Halloween- I wanna be like a Taelon from *Earth: The Final Conflict*."

"Hair status can change. You never know." I stared at his cigarette to see how long we'd have to be in the cold. He was shivering a bit.

Then he sputtered: "I'm not gay anymore."

He was kinda throwing me here. That was a more abrupt subject switch than even he was usually guilty of.

"What do you mean?"

"Well I have no desire for sex anymore- at all. So I guess that makes me un-gay."

"That makes you celibate, not un-gay."

I didn't want to argue with him. The chemo had smoothed out his skin and made him fuzzy, like an out-of-focus ghost. Although the cocktail had erased HIV from his blood, the cancer was on a world tour invasion of his body. He was more Da'an than Kevin at that moment.

I was terrified of seeing him in the hospital during his treatments. He was in and out a lot. But I did visit him quite a bit though I know I wasn't doing all that I could have. It's the only thing I feel guilty about in my whole life. Maybe I am making a big deal about it. He probably didn't care too much if I was there. Although when I saw him at his mom's house there were all these pictures of his friends. My picture had a thumbtack through my forehead. Ouch.

His actress/would-be singer/muse Solange's image had a gold frame. It was a professionally snapped portrait.

"She sent it to me that way, framed up like that." he had explained. "I think she wanted to insure her picture had an appropriate venue."

"That's mildly controlling."

She seemed as bizarrely seductive and as dangerously exotic as all the demonic hookers, circus freaks and undead vengeance seekers she had played in her Italian Giallo movies. He'd never told me how he had met her. I can only imagine the circumstances.

She didn't get to visit Kevin before he was found. At least he never mentioned her visiting. He was found at the beach before she came back from Europe. It was rumored she would put in a guest-starring appearance at graveside. I was anxious to meet her. It would be her last chance to say goodbye in grand style or at least with an audience that would appreciate it.

Kevin's exit demanded a few big names be in attendance.

From what they could tell he went to the beach, walked out as far as he could to the sand bar and pulled the trigger. I don't know how he got a gun. They hadn't found it with him. Maybe it had been dragged end over end by the tide down into nowhere. The missing gun made a lot of people's eyes roll but to me it simply added to Kevin's mystique. He would attain a strange local legend status on Cape Cod. Kevin and his missing clues. I had a weird vision of it lying on the bottom of the ocean off Marconi Beach with a stream of bubbles coming from the barrel.

A Pisces child to the end. We were both Pisces. Two fish, like the symbol from the zodiac- one swimming up, one swimming down.

I was swimming in place, just slowing down slightly to attend this graveside ceremony. The cemetery was over-green with summer flowers, wreaths, and little signs for war veterans encrusted with red, white, blue and silver stars. It made me think of what it would look like on a full moon night, under twice frozen snow. Kevin's stone wasn't there yet.

The sun, however, was. It had finally come out from behind a week long cloud cover. It was truly hot now, not just the unfocused muggy that had vagued out all my mixed emotions about today. It was a concentrated, sharp-rayed sun- the kind that forces you to pay attention because it hurts your eyes so much. And I didn't need much more prompting. I had to really concentrate in order to figure out where I was supposed to stand. Hung over or non-smoking?

On one side of the casket was all of Kevin's pre- and post- palliative care suburban family and on the other side were all his crazy chic friends from the city dressed like models and prostitutes- because they were. Both sides did their best to communicate but mostly it was like one of those first contact scenarios from Star Trek, which made it kind of unpredictable and exciting. It was as ultra-glamorous as death could be. I cried and touched the casket just like a real Hollywood widow on American Movie Classics. The casket-side service was blink-quick. Everyone wanted it to be short to keep the public weeping to a minimum. Myself? I was overblown and lame but I knew that somewhere in one of those infinite infinities, Kevin loved my melodrama.

Candy was almost 5 feet tall. If there was ever a girl that should not have been named Candy- it was Candy. She was really butch. She was punk, like the toughest girl in school. Crew cut, short dyed-black hair and eyes that kinda two-hole-punched you.

I had this shirt back then with red stick figure reindeer printed on it like primitive French cave paintings. My hair was dyed blue-black and teased into this haystack (definitely not an organic experience) that got me nicknamed "Cure Boy" by the three straight-edge skins that went to my high school. I think it was the shirt that made Candy start talking to me. She stopped me in the hall to tell me it was a great pattern.

I thought she was the guide for cool. I hung out with her as much as possible. She smoked clove cigarettes and skipped classes all the time. She drove me to Nauset Light Beach where Kevin was sitting, watching the waves stretch the sunset out. I think she was trying to set us up. It didn't really work but we became friends. Kevin had wavy brown hair, seraph-esque. He always gave the impression that he had a secret he was just about to let you in on. Kinda hypnotic in a way that suspense held by the half-promise of being let in on a joke.

We were a bit shy about sex. Candy was really open about fucking. She was bisexual when most of us were virgins. Her boyfriend was a mortician and they would pick up girls together. Suburban legend was that one girl OD'd with them and they made it look like she had fallen down the stairs with the help of mortician Lee's grisly knowledge of the human body "when dead." All this was real rebellion back then. Now it just seems logical.

Candy wasn't at the funeral. Rumor was that she was living with a new guy somewhere in Texas in a trailer park. So much for rebellion. Hand me the TV Guide.

Darla, however, was at the funeral. She had driven me there in her big jeep thing. Darla was a divorced mother of three who was probably closer to Kevin than I was at the time of his death. If close means hanging out with all the drag hookers he knew and mistakenly smoking crack with them.

I loved reminding her that she was my mom's age and she'd accidentally smoked crack with some transvestites that must have turned tricks just like Kevin. Such a carnival atmosphere. She smiled and with a decidedly Candy Darling-type voice said: "It was beautiful," She said 'beautiful' like she was spelling out the word, slow and intricately. "But then they said it was crack." She was one of those working single moms that Fox News always gets wrong. She had the directions to the cemetery written on the back of a credit card bill envelope. For as long I had known Darla she never wasted anything. She was one of the only people I knew that could recycle and still have a sense of style. She was the only mother of three that listened to Boards of Canada too, at least from her generation- that I knew of.

Immediately upon arrival Darla was absorbed into Kevin's drag coterie. They worshiped her. I simply stood to the side and watched the trannie procession of faux couture pull her into their midst.

I had a National Geographic when I was little that had drawings of all the things that happened at a typical bigwig funeral in Ancient Egypt. The paid mourners standing around with pats of perfumed wax melting on top of their braided wigs. The columns of mourners, the ceremonial declarations and decorations. Darla was like Liz Taylor in *Cleopatra* sans lapis lazuli, sans "White Diamonds."

"They found him on the beach." She proclaimed softly to the synthetically coiffed throng, smoothing a mascara infused tear across her cheek with the back of her left hand leaving a sad glamour line. Everyone had heard this before a million times, but when Darla talked she made it seem like a re-enactment. She was a special effects master.

A mighty Afro-dite chirped into our ears: "I didn't know he was so hooked on drugs. He was doing coke like crazy." Darla nodded, more tears slid down dark lines. "I have to admit I was a bit naive about a lot of his life. He kept things hidden, but not that well hidden."

"I know, I know." chimed someone who obviously didn't.

How could they with that hairstyle?

"Hello to you too." Darla greeted more people I had never met or seen before. Kisses, hugs, her hands were always warm and dry. "He certainly didn't need a drug to trip. Poor sweet baby." She seemed a little tired of the attention. I gave her a quick look that meant "please don't introduce me to anyone." We had met 12 years ago through an ex-show-stopping, showboat ex-boyfriend during a summer stock run of Grease. It was a ritual that she would drive me to big milestones in our lives. I used to joke that she couldn't die before me because then I wouldn't have a ride to her funeral.

Driving was a phobia of mine. After Kevin got diagnosed (and immediately hospitalized, the first of many such incarcerations) he begged me to get tested, quit smoking and to get my driver's license finally- all in that order. So I got tested and quit smoking. I haven't done the license yet. I've convinced myself that driving would be a bad thing for me to be able to do. I didn't trust myself with that much metal. The breeze had picked up. The old ladies that had worn hats suddenly realized why no one did anymore.

Kevin's mother appeared in front of me. I could feel the big camera lens of God focus on me. Everyone there was watching her every minute of this public ritual. I fell into her gravitational embrace. Her lips to my ear: "He's in a much better place now John, you know it." She held me out before her with both hands, smiling. She was a busty blond with the word 'party' perpetually on the tip of her tongue, next to the Virginia Slim.

Even in these past few soul destroying months I hadn't seen her breakdown. I had sat in her kitchen, Kevin upstairs in his room lying down, while she explained that there wasn't anymore that could be done. I was with friends but she stared at me, into my eyes. I don't know what she saw there. I only felt like someone had shut off my heart.

I don't think she had anymore tears; she'd burned out her crying fuse. I smiled back at her, into the hot summer breeze and, seemingly spurred on by my expression, she whirred away- into another group of sad curious people. I stared at my reflection in the surface of Kevin's shiny coffin handles.

And then I saw Solange. Well, first her reflection in the coffin. She was behind me. A different sort of camera lens leveled on me. I turned around and looked up at her, into the future. The future appeared black, stylish and impossibly thin.

Solange was couture, calm, collected and striking at the grave: Vivica A. Fox with a dash of Darth Vader. She wore a shiny black suit, made of some high tech Italian synthetic. Molto non-stick. She had positioned herself so that everyone could see the hot dry wind rip through her hair. Even though it was in short dreadlocks and clung to her head like a hennaed tarantula. She caught my eyes and came towards me. She knew exactly who I was, as if she had been the one to see all my movies.

As she introduced herself to me she stubbed a cigarette out on her heel. It was like a heroine had stepped out of a Creature Double Feature matinée and into my life, or more accurately, she had suddenly cast me in some bit part in hers.

"I'm Solange."

"I know. I've always wanted to meet you. I'm John."

She was the only statuesque African-American eighties' Italian horror movie actress there. It would have been hard not to know who she was. Her eyes got all fiery and kinda caramelized.

"Kevin told me so many things about you." Awkward

pause, square Gucci-ish lighter to another Dunhill Red- ignite, drag, puff. A big chunk of multi-carat ice made a squelchy cold bling at my eyes in the warm sunlight- then got hidden again under her cuff as she slipped the lighter back into her pocket. "And now here we are."

"It seems strange that we never met before." I went into that awkward third person personality-mode I get when I am not sure what to do or how to talk to someone. I act like a strange puppet of myself manipulated by someone else. A caricature that talks in a stilted way too. Nice for the first impressions, huh?

"Not really. Kevin liked to keep his friends in different boxes. You weren't in my box, sweetheart."

Umm, owww- this of course made me curious. What box had I been in? Was I the boring childhood friend box? The safety deposit box? I wanted to not be jealous about this kind of stuff. But she was forcing me.

"We were friends since we were 15."

"I know. So how do you feel?"

"Angry I guess."

"Yeah, me too. I wonder what that means."

Early on I thought I would become a shrink. I figured I had been trying to sort out my own head so long that other peoples' heads would be child's play. But then I woke up to the reality of how much school that is and how much that school costs- and how much I hate listening to people yammering on about their problems. Chronic whiners have no place in my life. Now I was almost thirty and had done the incredibly extensive groundwork for an interesting career as an overly cultured temp.

"I feel like shit."

"Me too. I was in Europe when all this went down and I couldn't visit. I was caught at loose ends, but things worked out- I mean they worked out that I could get here. Not that anything really worked out.

Another awkward, yet delicious pause.

"That's a beautiful suit." Duh.

"I only wear Prada to funerals. I think that is what it is made for." Yeah, if all funerals were held on the *Battlestar Galactica*.

"You saw him in and out of the hospital?" She said hospital like it was a foreign language word she had just picked up and was unsure of its proper use.

"Yeah. I hated going but I did it."

"Yeah, well no one loves hospitals. He was so young. In all ways."

"Yeah."

Solange and I stared at the crowd as it dissolved into cars. She turned to me with an expression I had seen before in her movies, usually after she had been stung, irradiated or bitten by something that would later mutate her.

"Hey John, this is kind of a weird request but do you think I could stay with you a few days? I don't have anyone here anymore now that Kevin's gone and I don't plan on staying too long- just as long as the ticket back. So maybe we could hang out. Maybe have a little party time for Kevin, make him proud, you know? If you have the space, of course."

"Of course, that would be fun." I was so thrilled I almost jumped out of my skin. I so wanted to mutate too.

For some reason she was eager to make a connection with me- I figured it had to do with a bit of guilt at not seeing Kevin before the big event. I think everyone ends up feeling that way in a suicide. I was feeling a bit guilty myself, but more than eager to hang out with her and absorb her fabulousness through my pores. She made me feel like I was going to take Kevin's place in her heart, wherever that was.

Darla drove Solange and me back to my apartment, sort of staring at the two of us, giving Solange the 'extraterrestrial look.' I don't think Darla liked her much- 'vampire Nefertiti' doesn't sound too much like a compliment.

I slept on the pullout couch. She slept in my bed but kept her clothes in the living room.

"To give you space when you have to change for work."

Later that night I cried myself to sleep listening to *Four Calendar Café* by the Cocteau Twins. I don't think she heard me.

One thing about me that was always off-putting for new friends and lovers was my 'luck.' That's what my mom calls it but when she says 'luck' I think she's encoding the word violence. Violence has always been around me. It was a noticeable trait, like the small off-color spot in the white of my left eye.

I was born in a hospital that had just started to burn down. I was five years old when the first gun was pulled in my presence. I was eleven when I saw my first dead body outside of a wake-, which happened when I was 9. By the age of 13 I had been in two car accidents, a bank robbery and had fallen off a bridge. Nothing physical permanently damaged but I can't say that about my personality.

I was about eleven when I discovered my tear ducts- it was during a bout of 'mirror face,' what Kevin and I called acting melodramatic in front of the mirror alone. I actually realized they were little holes at the inside edges of my eyes- it freaked me out. What a fucking strange thing. And what an amazingly tiny set of weapons. I used them. I wasn't a whiny kid but I got what I wanted. I think I got away with a lot because I was always some sort of weird victim of unbelievable crimes and collisions.

If my life was a TV movie of the week I would want the opening credits to roll with Gary Numan's "Cars" playing over them. Not because I'm a big fan of automobiles (as you well know)or Gary Numan for that matter, but because I love the sound of those falling synthesizer chords. It reminds me of coming down an escalator and into camera view. And here I am, giving the camera a butch yet sultry pout. Lots of chrome and glass and plexi would shine around me and digital readouts would be superimposed on the images. As if I lived in a space station. Devoid of human contact.

In fact, I'd like "Are Friends Electric" on the soundtrack of my life too. Love those mounting chords filling the air with icy omniscience.

"The key to everything is relaxation. Deep breaths." So my mother said if I had a crying jag. My childhood wasn't a place for relaxation. It was an ice cube in the sun. OK, an ice cube made of Zarex, in the sun.

Violence (or actually the aftermath- which is really the worst part) was always near me or lingering around me. I'm not bragging or trying to seem tough and worldly. I'm more like the wrong person in the wrong place at the right time. Darla loved taking me to the mall. She was always convinced that something would blow up. I am convinced she is a closet looter.

I haven't decided if it is something I do or something I actually am. I only know that it is something that can be counted on. One of the only things in my life so far that is clock-like precise, (that and my coffeemaker.) I had even started to almost enjoy it.

I didn't explain my violence thing to Solange. I wanted a new someone with new opinions of me. I wanted a break from the that reputation, I guess. I figured with her I could bury the old me with Kevin.

"See, it's a really sexually charged work but it's emotionally desperate. She's had her heart broken and…"

"Broken by who?" Solange was sitting on my couch, red wine in left hand, tipsy, dissecting my cd collection. In her right hand was the case for a copy of Madonna's *Erotica* that had seen much wartime duty as a coaster. Solange was a big talker. She loved to sit and talk about art and music all day and all night. What was really cool was that she actually knew a lot of people worth talking about. But not Madonna. She hadn't broken into that orbit yet.

"Sean, Ingrid, Warren, Sandra? It doesn't matter- what matters is how well she makes all the pieces fit together."

"Go on." I tapped the side of my wine glass lightly in rhythm to the song playing. I had just bought the stereo, it was a new Panasonic with a mirrored front that looked almost clinical in its futurism.

"Well, she's had her heart broken, she doesn't believe in love anymore- she's gonna go out and fill up on all this sex and sensation and the hell with love because her faith in it is totally gone. She wants sleazy good times."

"Doesn't explain the *Sex* book."

"Yeah in a weird way it does- she's trying to fill all the senses. She's trying to blot out the sadness- of her lack of faith and hope. That's what leads her through the cd. And you know what the key is? You know why I was freaking out when I first heard this cd?"

"No, tell me." Tell me, you totally amazing gay man's muse.

"In the song "Erotica" she's singing about all this B&D and shit but there's this word she keeps repeating like a mantra, in an almost questioning voice. Romance."

"Sounds a little out of place."

"It's what led me to understand the cd. A lot of people refuse to see Madonna as an artist. They slag her off as a slut or a businesswoman- both actually. It's stupid because she is really a lot more interesting. Regardless, you don't get the feeling that something is really wrong until around "Bye Bye Baby" where she's pissed and bitter about the heartbreaker. Then by "Deeper and Deeper" she's singing about how she put her trust in something and it bit her and she doesn't believe in it now and how she went the wrong way. And she needs to get back to love and be true to what her dad and mom told her."

"Even if she has to pose nude with a gang bang of lesbian skinheads to do it." I got up and pulled the cd sleeve out of her hands and looked at the artwork. The paper was wrinkled from being wet and then having dried inside the plastic case. I bought *Erotica* when it first came out; I was living in San Francisco. It seemed really cold and crafted. Even if she was sucking someone's toes.

"And "Bad Girl" is like the ultimate *Woman Under The Influence* dance song. Doesn't it remind you of.."

"Of Kevin in college- and me in college actually."

"OK well- I guess everyone has their own take- the really cool part is on the last bonus track, "Secret Garden", she's ready to be reborn- she's ready to give it another go."

"Yeah, I always liked that song."

"It's amazing what heartbreak can achieve. It's fuel for the artist. Put heartbreak to beats and you have a hit. She's awesome." Solange was preaching to the converted. Drunkenly.

She had a smiley face on now, I hadn't seen her smile before. At least in real life- she had smiled like an evil blood drenched banshee in her horror films but this was different. Now I had the *Queen of Hell* grinning in my living room (in the sequel at least- "I did my own stunts in that one," she later confided.)

"I have always agreed that Madonna is the ultimate pop artist. You'll get no argument from me there. But I still like the 82-84 look best, the black rubber bracelets and the low tide hair. I love that. It reminds me of high school. She was kinda working punk into disco." No wonder a lot of people hated her.

"Um she was almost Goth with those crosses. She sang new wave-resuscitated disco and dressed like a slutty Bauhaus fan. Perfect."

More wine. More wine.

"Hey her brother cruised me at a restaurant once in Los Angeles. Nice eyes, big head. Like the Madonna prototype v.1"

"So what do you get out of this? What's the message?"

"This is a themed recording, a concept album, not about sex and sluttiness like everyone is always saying. It's a concept album about a bitter, heartbroken woman who is about to be re-born. Into self-awareness, adulthood maybe and perhaps even real love."

"And you are on the same trajectory? Where's the little Roccos and Lourdes?"

"Just watch- just watch out for the next guy I date."

"Huh?"

"Watch for when my life changes. If you know the cycles you can anticipate what's going to happen next."

"That sounds kinda boring."

We had drunk obviously too much, ended up sitting on the floor of my bedroom. She suddenly blurted out about the job idea.

"Do you want to work for me? Be like a production assistant slash personal assistant? In Europe this fall and maybe winter?"

"Yeah!"

"I'm gonna do this guerrilla video lifestyle food magazine show. It'll involve reviewing food and meeting owners of different restaurants in Europe. You can help with the odds and ends of it all. I'm sure they'll be a lot of stuff to do. And I pay very well. All expenses etc."

I had a lot of experience with putting together video and photo shoots from all my half-jobs and career mis-starts along the way. I had gone to college for a vague degree in something nebulous like "communications." A catch-all really.

"I've done a show like this already in Northern Ireland. Now is the time to do one that really captures the un-tourist view of Europe. That's my big keyword for this whole thing, word du jour. 'Un-tourist.' I might even call it *The Un-Tourist Guide.* I want it to be the kind of places that the locals go to. The authentic taste of a certain town. Not the homogenized version, we're going for nc-17 food- no trumped up PG phony tourist shit. No EPCOT sanitized Times Square. Not dives though, just hip funky shite, ya know? No acid wash denim revivals thanks."

"Sounds cool." Sounded really cool, traveling around Europe eating, as a full time job? I was depressed and my temping was leading to a life of transience. Maybe it was even a boot camp for what she was offering. I didn't really believe anything she said but it sounded like a boredom-killer. It might have been that she felt like this could make up for something with Kevin too. Again, my mantra was she's paying for the flight and the hotel. I was escaping. She was paying for everything, the plane, and the place to stay.

That was it. We went back into a weird, almost religious, solemnity. That was ok. I was settling into the whole mood, the vibe that Solange was projecting. She knew just as much as I did that she was a bit over the top, and it added something to her whole mystique.

I wanted a change, so I was even more willing than usual to encourage that kind of behavior. I guess I wanted to get some revenge against something, fate whatever. I wanted to get back at all the clean living robots that had turned away from Kevin- maybe myself included. Get to know more people like him, become like him, in some small way. Live on for him; take up where he left off. And that would be a trip with Solange, his mysterious muse, a woman who had shuffled him through Europe just after college with all the fanfare of an African-American Auntie Mame.

She began to organize her stuff. Most of it had exploded out of her leather luggage and into my living room. Hair stuff, a lot of expensive clothes. She was into Prada for shoes, and Gucci everything, lots of black viscose jersey with a pseudo-Missoni thing hunched and bunched on my coffee table that I figured was a sweater- she hadn't worn it around me. Maybe it was just too hot for it.

She used the same cream deodorant as my mom. Weird.

When I got home later in the afternoon most of it was packed up in her Louis Vuittons. This I took as a clue that we'd be going soon.

She had abandoned some facial scrub and some fancy girlie shaving cream in my shower. I used it. It smelled like over-ripe fruit- so much so that I thought it had gone bad somehow.

I could smell it as I toweled dry.

By the time I had gotten out of the bathroom she had already split. She left a little note ("Honey here's the lowdown.") and two hundred Euros hair-clipped to a printed Expedia itinerary for me on the kitchen table. The note gave me the hotel I was supposed to stay at if for some reason she couldn't meet me at the airport. It already had reservations for me. I probably should have questioned why she hadn't wanted to travel together but I was pretty excited and I liked traveling alone anyway. And besides, she had already left anyway.

I dripped from the shower, shivered in the end of the day summer air. I shook it off- whatever was coming up, I was prepared to let it happen- even if that's all I could do.

My whole life up to this point had been this game of prove-me-wrong. I'd been setting up myself to see if it would fall apart. That's hard to explain. It's like I refused to believe that the world could possibly function in a way contrary to how I believed it does. That, perhaps, good things do happen without karmic strings, sometimes I am proven wrong- but usually not. At least I tend to not see it that way- which in itself must be a symptom of something. And of course if something good does happen it, in itself, also serves to throw me for a loop as I don't know what to do with a good thing. I was now determined to try. Going to Europe and working with Solange out of the blue might be what I needed. The question that really needed answering though, the one I conveniently did not make a stab at was, the proverbial: why me?

I wanted my meeting her to be a spark in my whole dry existence. I was going through my life thinking that I could plan everything out- but it turns out that some arbitrary chance encounter was really what got me moving in a direction. That's really living- the random chance.

Kevin's death really was a weird switch that channeled some of his crazy energy to me. I can't be really sure how random his death was but it was unexpected. I had thought we had passed the hurdle of AIDS safely wrapped in latex. I thought we had beaten those odds. Hooking up with Solange was my big flourish in risk taking, was my big chance to flip the bird to whatever future was being cobbled for me. Fuck destiny.

I figured it was time to stop playing it safe. There is a point where self-preservation actually becomes self-destruction. I believed that there is a point in your life that, if you don't throw yourself into your life, you end up left behind. You end up on the wrong train headed to no-where land - or worse, dead. I suppose there could be a person, a place or a thing holding you back too. There could also be a person, place or thing that forces you to come into focus. Regardless- it's important to know when to let go. It's important to know when to stop holding onto your heart.

I passed a hand through my hair, brushed my teeth and got dressed in some sober lightweight suit. Coffeemaker was preprogrammed, magically produced a decent brew. It was probably the only dependable thing I had in my life. Sad huh? Boo-hoo.

Fully caffeinated, I went down to the curb to wait for my Super Shuttle to grim, gray, concrete Logan Airport.

The world reboots in my head whenever I land in an airplane. Just one second of static and then a popping kind of sound and the sky will come back on blue and clean- ready to accept more travelers or stars or weather, what-have-you's.

I fear flying, but not how you might think. I've flown a lot. My parents had jobs that had taken me all around when I was younger. So it wasn't the plane itself really. I was used to the ritual. I loved taking off and even landing. The part I feared was the part of human beings that can shut off the worry and get inside a machine like that and travel x miles an hour for x hours at x thousands of feet. Pretend it's 'just a bus- but in the sky' like my mom cheerily used to say? I guess we have to if we're going to go anywhere but it's still scary to think that the human brain can remove itself so completely from the sheer unnatural sense of flying in a big bullet full of gas through the sky.

I am afraid of myself in that respect. I mean, how can anyone get in a plane if they really think of the concept? OK, I was getting way ahead of myself- because unfortunately- this plane had not landed yet and now I had to add up all the aisle numbers again in my head. It's something I do unconsciously a lot and I always wondered if it was a sign of mental illness. I have to look that up.

58-59-60. I counted again and looked over at the windows. The windows of planes fascinate me. For some reason they remind me of whales. Like blow holes or something. I know it doesn't make sense but that is the image and the feeling I get when I look at them.

The plane popped an air pocket and went into that "Doesn't it feel like we're going to plummet to our moist yet squished yet charred death" thing it does so well. I shifted on the tiny chair.

I supposed I was handsome in that John Garfield-ish way that I like. Culprit, not convict- and Garfield always reminded me of a cross between Jimmy Cagney and James Dean so that works for me. I stared at the plane blow hole window and put my cheek against it long enough to make the woman in the facing aisle notice. 'I'm strange' she mentally made a note of me. I did it too. When I get in a crowd I size up all the people and stick the mental post-it on all their foreheads. "Big dumpy salt shaker-shaped lady" would be scrawled on her day-glow pink label.

The trip would have been enjoyable but I had to smell the airline food the whole time and that nauseates me and fills me with dread at the same time. There is nothing worse than stale food odors and noisy co-travelers. Or foreboding.

Regardless, I could feel the plane do its turn that signals to all frequent fliers that the destination was near. The pilot was going to attempt to bring the thousands of pounds down in one piece, shiny and innocent- all-who-me? I've-never-been-40,000 feet in the air.

The sun blasted into the cabin as we tilted in the air. The ground below us filled up to the horizon seams with quaintness. Green hills, little French cars, little French houses. Little French clouds pulled mini-shadows across the profiles of these buildings and ponds for dramatic effect. My Discman (which of course should not have been switched on during take-off and landing) provided as much high-blown-drama-soundtrack as the Psychedelic Furs were ever capable of. Which was plenty- in case you were wondering.

Charles De Gaulle is a wacky airport, even more so now with all the security. Traveling through there numerous times I'd basically skipped through the checkpoints because the plane was so late. No such luck anymore. Now the flight was late because of the security. Anyway, it was a blue turning to gray day when I arrived. The clouds became thick, choking the airport in dirty towels.

Paris limp-wristed a damp cool blue morning to greet my arrival at CDG. But it also gave me Solange, waiting in the airport lobby, a sentinel of glamorous glamour- with more secrets than even her eye-popping appearance could ever insinuate. However, her smile was warm, real- and just beyond the last security checkpoint.

In the cab from CDG Solange got all technical. I felt like a shrink-wrapped head hunter victim.

"So what kind of camera should we get- I want it shot all guerrilla style."

"I guess we'll have to get all that somewhere here."

"Somewhere here or in Italy. No, here because then we can test it out on some place here. It's up to you. I don't think we will do anything in Paris this visit. We'll come back. Now we should concentrate on soaking up some good atmosphere. But you should be thinking about the stuff we'll need- just lightweight high quality stuff. And give me a budget on what it will cost."

"Can do."

"OK so what do you want to do? I want to shop, but that is what I always want to do. And I have some friends I want to visit. Crazy fun friends you may or may not like. Parisians either love you or don't think about you. I like that."

"Sounds good." I was still in some sort of shock that I was in Paris and that I had called my temp job to tell them to fuck off. I guess it was starting to sink in that I was on my own--or as on my own as I could be with Third Female Victim from *Decapitator*

2 as my boss.

"Are you excited? Sorry I didn't fly with you. I have this phobia and I couldn't get your tickets on the same flight anyway."

"Phobia? About flying together?"

"I know its very Saudi royal family but yeah- it's a quirk."

"O-K."

"Anyway- are you excited?"

"Yes, very." But I am sure that I didn't look excited. I think I looked like runny yogurt.

"You just need to chill out and rest and get used to my world!" Solange said with a flourish of hands that made all her bracelets clang and clash like mini-gongs. She seemed like ancient priestess with all her accoutrements and the way she was gesticulating. Maybe she was trying to purge my fear.

"I'll be fine- sometimes flying doesn't agree with me. I feel like my stomach is inside out."

"It could have been the airport food. No problem. Just relax and enjoy. Our hotel is on the next street."

Paris is the city that movies got wrong for me. I'd been there two times before. History like that doesn't translate as picture book, theme park or zoo; the equation doesn't work. In Florida during that long hot summer of my last ignorance to reality I had argued with my dad about the EPCOT Eiffel Tower. I wanted to get there- I wanted to go up in it. Of course, this is impossible. The tower at EPCOT is a tiny replica set up to look like the Eiffel Tower in the distance. It's an American dream metaphor set on a little phony Parisian set.

Solange had a favorite hotel in Paris that was pricey but located just close enough to the spots to be handy. I had to share a room with her—-not because she didn't want to pay for another one for me--there just wasn't any free at the moment.

"Location is essential."

The heat in the room was on for some reason. It was raising the dead, old cigarette smells from the drapes, although everything looked clean and bright. I had to unplug the malfunctioning heater/air conditioning unit to achieve earth atmosphere. I couldn't even feel that foreign. I felt weirdly at home. The room reminded me of my grandparents. Since I had given up smoking the smell of cigarettes in hotel rooms reverted back to memories of my grandparents and trips to Maine with them. Those were great days. My grandfather worked for the government. I never really found out doing what but it allowed for some long term traveling all around. He would take my grandmother and me for weeks at a time and I would be like a prince on tour.

I became versed in the quirks of hotels at the age of eight. Traveling was not a weird experience for me. I loved getting away. Sometimes there would be kids at the hotels and we'd hang out and stare at each other by the pool or the ice machine. Transient friendships.

The ice machine was a truly ominous device. It was usually where it always is, down the hall like some goblin with a big cold mouth full of broken teeth. Sometimes my grandmother would entrust me with the ice run and I would go out to the machine and scoop out the ice chunks into a little cardboard container that always reminded me of Kentucky Fried Chicken.

When my grandparents moved to Florida we went to Disney. My grandfather retired from his government job but still wanted to be somewhere close to the NASA launches (but not too close) so they got a house in Daytona Beach. Every afternoon it would rain hard and their backyard would get all silvery green and the lizards would hide under the pots and storm drains. When they first moved in I found tiny skeletons in the multi-louver windows. Lizards trapped between the glass that had starved. Probably even cooked first because the sun would beat on those tiny see-through cells and fry them. The bones were really delicate and beautiful, like some miniature Smithsonian dinosaur. Sad for an 11 year old to see. I cleaned them out with a small brush that my grandmother gave me. More evidence to get rid of. Used to that.

It was really close to the beach and my brother and I would walk there every morning after doing some chores like mowing the lawn or taking out some trash. We were staying with them for a few months while my parents worked out what they were going to buy for a new house. Amazingly- they never asked our opinions on the house they bought.

So we'd spend a lot of time on the beach turning brown and swimming. Our lives up north disappeared into history as if they had been yet to be discovered.

I feel bad for anyone who hasn't visited the real Paris.

Solange had begun to unpack her bags. I took the opportunity to go into the bathroom and see what the plane ride had done to my face. Maybe even get a shower before Solange fructified the whole place with her shampoos and scrubs

"I'm going to the Champs Elysee Sephora to calm myself down." She was futzing with the new SIM card of her GSM phone. Finally she tapped it into place and slid the phone shut.

"Are you stressed about something? Not me right?" I shouted from the bathroom.

"Oh no honey. I just like to say that because it's a good excuse to spend money. I'll go out and get some aromatherapy and sit in the bathtub for a million years. They have everything at this store. It's like a big piece of Christmas fell out the sky."

Solange's resume was actress slash model slash singer and it started somewhere in 1985. My kind of people. She had a faint kind of dance hit in the prior West Germany -hence her love of things Berlin.

"I guess I am still a bit desperately new wave, but Sephora has this shade of eye shadow that I used to wear in the

80's"

Her only sorta hit song was in Germany. It was called "Robots are Un-American." If you blinked you would have missed the cheapo Wendy O. Williams meets Grace Jones knock-off video she did for it with some fucked up anti-skinhead skinhead that ran a TV repair store on Bleibtreustrasse. I used to love the part where the screen split into panels and she had a conversation with herself in 4 parts- each version of her a different color with matching pipe cleaners. The fashion was strictly vinyl, rubber and trash bags. I think I was 12 at the time- she was 20.

"I really should get this framed, don't you think?? It's so dated now." Solange came into the bathroom with a tattered magazine page. "It was a really rancid 'fashion finds it's footing from the street' *Vogue* spread. I can't remember doing any of this."

"*Vogue* druggie!"

"I wish. I think that was when I was doing my 'I'm not a trannie- I just look like one" thing, and umm, lots of cocaine."

"Neat. Is there a reason that you brought all that stuff with you to a hotel?"

"Where am I supposed to store my stuff? And if my short film thing gets into Locarno then I will have a press kit for a film festival already here."

"Huh?"

"I did this short film and I sent it to some European film festivals. I haven't really completed it yet but it keeps getting better every time someone invests in it."

She popped it into the v.c.r. she had requested from the lobby.

It was like a really Euro car commercial, Solange getting out of a sleek shiny hunk of interstellar spacecraft in a pair of Gucci mules that clung to her feet as she pressed them down into the comet dusted tarmac. She was working this slicked-back hair thing that made me wish I was her luggage.

"The lead girl character has highly-detailed fantasies about getting off spaceships in couture clothing."

She mumbled something about me helping out with that too. I would have done it just to go to Locarno.

"I love Locarno." Mostly because of the Grand Hotel- it is so trashy/chic. It's the kind of place I'd like to imagine I belong in. I am not sure if film people take Solange seriously. I do know however that they take her to bed. Her appetite is well known in quite a few small European resort towns. Towns that feature that tan that she calls "warm leatherette."

Solange was rearranging her dreads when I came out of the shower. The dreads were a signature thing. People recognized her from the Giallo movies when she wore them. They would come up and say in Italian "You ate that man's eyeball while he was still alive!" Solange would laugh like she did in the movie and they'd clear out.

A few times she even scared the shit out of me. Her kind of beauty--and she is really beautiful which is why so many B-film horror movie guys want to make her a demon with deadly pus-oozing sores--relies on a bit of insanity to catalyze it visually, on the part of her and the beholder in equilibrium, I suppose. And of course there is the whole thing about seeing a person in a film before actually meeting them and their performance is mostly as a demon vampire woman who eviscerates her human prey. Kinda colors the moment.

The windows of our hotel room looked out towards the Eiffel Tower, hypodermically pressed against the cloud cover. Soothing pinks and oranges and dull stoked reds. Solange threw aside the drapes.

"Why does this kind of stuff always look so cheesy in photos but so beautiful in real life? Here it is all majestic and shit."

"Yeah it's really nice."

"Let's go spend some money."

Solange proceeded to lead me the scant crowded steps from rue Saint-Philippe du Roule to the Sephora on the Champs Elysee. It was like being inside a Captain and Tenille Christmas decoration from the seventies alright.

"How are you doing? Is it too much for you?" Solange had a basket of tiny perfume vials. Empty glass vials..

"For the crack?"

"No silly."

"Speed? Liquid LSD?

"I mix my own essential oils. These are really the only size that works for me."

"Okay, whatever you say. I am getting some Helmut Lang."

"Good choice. I love the smell of that stuff."

Solange puttered around a display of bath oils and soaps that look like the stain of a gay pride flag that had liquefied.

"Blueberry or lilac, lemon or sandalwood?"

"Whatever you like."

"You're going to have to smell it- they're strong."

"Lemon. So you are lemony fresh."

She undid a tester and sniffed. Her nose crinkled.

"Naw."

Solange's cell phone rang. It was a song I don't know.

"Hello." She listened intently and then laughed. "Ciao bella, si si, Parigi."

I poked through the colognes. Solange seemed to be having a one-sided conversation. She stood listening for almost two minutes just nodding.

"Va bene. Si, si. Ciao." She clicked the phone shut. "Well that's cool. I have to give some guys in Vienna a call. Never been there. About the show."

"Cool."

We checked out. Me with my bottle of Helmut Lang and Solange and her tiny empty perfume vials.

"Tomorrow we'll go pick up the camera and do a test. Okay?"

"Sounds good." It didn't seem like work yet at all.

Buying the video camera was actually fun. The store was like a French Best Buy, their version of loud colors and big speakers. Solange listened to everything that I had to say about each model and then she consistently picked the most expensive one.

"Why is this one five hundred more Euros than that one?"

"Um, there's more features. Longer battery life."

"Let's get that one."

I didn't have to try to sell her on dream equipment. She wanted to spend money. I think she wanted me to be happy with a new toy too.

"Does it come with a great bag? Or should we get a cool bag for it? What do you think." As she said this she handed the camera back to me and passed in front of a bank of cameras that fed images to a large plasma display for the front of the store. She didn't notice it but people had begun to stare at the screens. Who was this woman?

"Look." I motioned to the screen.

"Wow." She stepped back to get further into frame. "That is so cool. How much are these?"

"Really expensive and we don't need it."

"Yeah, imagine dragging that around Europe."

"We'd need a van. That's a big investment to just watch TV."

The five or six people who had been staring at the plasma screen suddenly realized that they were not watching a show, that Solange was actually a few yards from them. They all turned away from the image quickly with red faces.

"But wait, the show isn't over!" Solange spun around in front of the cameras. She tripled our expenses by smashing into three video cameras with her extended flash dance. "It's just beginning."

I slept forever. When I got up I was alone in the room. There was a note on the bathroom door. I was to discover that Solange's idea of p.a.'ing was meeting her for lunch at Costes after torrid couture shopping excursions. According to her note, she was out raiding the Comme De Garçon store somewhere on rue du Faubourg-St-Honoré, playing tag with the little red square robots there. I was to "soak in the French vibe and meet her around 2 at the Hotel Costes."

Costes was the kind of place that record labels made cd compilations about. You'd get a disc and a half of jazzy doodles on a mid-tempo beat with visions of sexy French evenings with Milla Jovovich sticking to the bar. I got there early and sat in the courtyard with a Caipirinha near a twosome that reminded me of leather bound library books splattered with day-glow paint. They spoke English so I was pretty much forced to listen to them.

"It wasn't the way he said I love you." This one was tanned like an animal hide. She was addressed as Cassie. Cassie had a Chanel bag the size of a VW propped next to her chair. A pair of big chunky 80's DJ headphones sat in her lap, completing her mummified Cheryl Tiegs look.

"Oh. Then what was it?" This other one thought she was Bjork at 55. Plastic surgery had left a wide-eyed anime sheen to her face.

"It was the amount of money it cost him to take the time to say it."

"A jet is *that* expensive?"

"Yeah I think so."

"Well just don't get pregnant and you wont have to worry about it."

"Oh I know- we'd have such ugly kids."

"Why do you say that?"

"My mother thinks so."

"Your mother knows about him?"

"She calls him Three Quarter Fox. It's a term for someone who's almost gorgeous and the parts of them that aren't so gorgeous make them even more desirable. But you can't count on a personality with kids. Who knows how they'll end up. Oh god!"

Cassie abruptly jerked her hand and fork away from her salad. The headphones slid down to the tiled floor with a clack.

"There is dirt on this salad- sir. Yes you- could you come here and look at this? It's dirt and it's on my salad."

"I am sorry miss- let me get the…"

"Well how about some forks and spoons and a new salad."

"Cassie chill, gees."

Cassie had the kind of face that never failed to remind

me that people have sphincters.

"I am gonna make such a huge scene."

"Please don't Cassie, please." Bjork-ette was getting desperate to avoid a messy drama row at Costes.

Cassie coiled up like an airbrushed cobra ready to strike into the deepest heart of all over-priced hip Parisian model traps when fancy my surprise, Solange flounced in and said hi to me- and to Cassie. The salad suddenly became lost as the soundtrack in my mind abruptly swelled to revolve around this meeting of the once-were-models. The thing to remember here is that Solange, out of the three, could easily still be modeling. And that was obvious to us, and the entire restaurant for that matter.

Cassie and Solange examined each other in a microsecond. A slowed down spy cam videotape of this altercation/chance meeting would reveal observational behaviors as scientific as any astronomer or biologist would employ. To the untrained eye this would have simply gone by as a flourish of cheek kissing and wardrobe straightening. To me it was a kind of dance that usually ended with happy vultures decloaking to circle dance.

When the courtyard settled they began to relate their shared bibliography. They had once modeled together. At this closer conversational range, Cassie actually looked a lot like Ali MacGraw and then I remembered my mom saying at a commercial break during "The Winds of War" in 1983 that somehow, Ali MacGraw had once been confused with someone pretty and she had started in the business as a model.

Solange sat down and propped her many shopping bags against the base of the table. I could see that Yohji Yamamoto had been pillaged.

"This is Cassie, John." Solange made hand-shaking gestures.

"Hi."

"Hi John. I was wondering what you were doing here sitting all alone." Piranha swam into my head.

"I was just drinking. Waiting for my synapses to have difficulty recognizing each other."

"Darling, I live for that moment." Her hearty laugh-at-her-own-joke laugh was infectious and revealed whiter-than-God teeth. I was sure she'd been living in that moment quite a while.

"Ok, well I've got to tear him away from y'all! We've got biz to discuss."

"Solange- such the business woman!" This was the other one, the Bjork one. She was older and seemed to be occupying a parallel dimension that only cursively interfaced with our own. She excused this with the line "My contacts are giving me a helluva time." This gave away the fact that she had, at one time, been a slut-druggie in some high school somewhere in New Jersey.

"Ciao Solange-baby, call me sometime. I didn't even know you were in Paris." Cassie whipped her Fendi sunglasses onto her face like a lizard displaying defensive, colored scales.

"Cassie, you know? Neither did I- it's been a real blur-

one of those months." Solange turned slowly towards me. I got the waiter's attention.

"I need to go to Vienna for a few days. You ok with that?"

I looked at her, nodded somewhat incredulously and ordered another Caipirinha.

"I've got to talk with some people who may be backing the show. I'll leave a list of restaurants for you to check out as potential feature places. And money of course. You can look over the stuff we're going to shoot and make some notes."

"Cha-ching!" I guess the Caipirinha at Costes were worth it. "But we just got here."

"I know honey- you do the big Paris tour thing, check it out. I've been in Paris so much it's like the Louvre came on me."

Solange leaned in and brought her voice down. "That bitch Cassie- she'd suck your tonsils out through your dick."

I was 5 years old.

"What do you do with my tonsils once they take them out?"

"Come on, get into the gown." She was a real no-nonsense nurse, the kind that shouldn't be helping pre-sedated little kids into operating gowns.

"Tell me what they do? Can I have them?"

"Your mother is going to be very angry if you don't put on the OR gown."

"Tell me what you are going to do with my tonsils?" I almost shrieked that in a little spoiled brat voice. I think the inflamed tonsils stifled the effectiveness of the sound however.

"We burn them. We burn your tonsils up." She sighed and pointed to the bathroom with her left hand as she held out the OR gown with her right.

I was freaked out by that. I envisioned these two little tonsils huddled together crying as the flames licked them into ash. Of course, everything had eyes and little hands back then because I watched too many cartoons so it was like the Holocaust for these poor little tonsils. I was always feeling sorry for myself I guess. I didn't want them to take a part of me out and toss it away. That nurse was a bitch.

"I don't want to wear the blue thing."

"You have to."

"Why do I have too?"

"If you don't wear this you have to go to the surgery naked." She pushed it at me like a straitjacket. Even as a 5 year old I thought they were kinky- with the bottom that could be removed. And I already knew why I had to wear it anyway. I was just testing her patience.

My blood would get everywhere.

"Get a nice close-up of that lobster John. Make it look like it's about to crawl off the plate." Solange was standing over the table about ready to jump down the lobster's throat if she could. I zoomed into the lobster and did a little dance with the camera. The light was making it gleam.

"We'll fix this stuff up in post."

One time in Maine my grandparents took me to a fancy (to me at the time) restaurant. I was obsessed with having a lobster. Just because I thought it was so weird looking. My grandfather was convinced that I wouldn't eat it. I argued with him until he ordered it for me. I was 6. My grandmother was pretty smart. She told my grandfather not to order anything for himself buy a burger from the kid's menu. Of course, when the big red spider monster was delivered to the table I immediately balked at the idea of eating it and switched plates with granddad.

Solange's idea of un-tourists spots was weird because this restaurant on rue du Colisée was featured in the hotel's special deals coupon book. She seemed to know everyone there too so I guess whatever works for her is fine with me.

This bald waiter guy was drumming the table with his fingers so loudly I almost said something, but I knew that it would only give Solange another excuse to say:

"We'll fix it in post, honey. Isn't this exciting, it's Jean Cocteau's restaurant."

"Yeah." It was. It was art-deco mixed with some wacky *Dr. Who* vibe. Red on red on red. I tried to refocus on the lobster while bald waiter guy continued to tap. I took Solange aside.

"That guy's tapping so loud I can hear it in the sound we're getting."

"No biggie, this is M.O.S. babe, M.O.S."

So far I had shot nothing but M.O.S., picture that would not have its synced sound utilized in the final cut. In post, as it were.

"What about your introduction speech stuff? You're going to have to talk." I wanted to say that this wasn't an Italian movie, we aren't going to dub everything and everyone.

"John, I know, of course. If its too noisy in here we can shoot it outside." Outside was practically under the Arc de Triomphe, cacophonous at this hour.

"Your wish is my command."

"Hey." She put her hand on my shoulder. "Don't get strung out on this John. I mean, you're doing a great job and I really appreciate your concern on the quality control and stuff, but I assure you, we can fix all this in post and have some really great footage. It's Paris, oui? Plus this is the trial run, so no biggie. Just film something, do whatever."

Through the open window I could smell all the new asphalt that those orange jumpsuits with pneumatics had laid out like a black carpet in front of the hotel. Metallic anisette soldered on a blast of scorched Parisian summer wind. It smacked into my sinuses with a dull, dry throb- made dub of my brainwaves. And, of course, that put me in such a piss poor mood that I wanted to rip the head off anything I could get my hands on. But then I re-remembered I had to meet Solange later today before she left for Vienna and I was lucky the jerks had gotten me out of bed. I was almost late. Fuck.

I got into the shower and lay in the cool tub. Hot water hit me like a million kisses. It almost always does the trick. Headache slacked, my head got a bit thinner, less stabbed.

I shut the shower off and flipped around with my feet to find the sandals on the bath mat. Out of the tub- still wet and looking in the mirror, I threw an assortment of grimacing reflections. I can do a great impression of sincerity in the bathroom. 'Mirror face.' Modeling for magazines that will never come out. The only subscription was in my own mind. Modeling, argh. More later.

I caught Kevin doing this a lot when we lived together. He stood in the bathroom doing commercials for Aveda products. He loved all that bio-essence beauty shit. Anything that smelled bosky or looked like dried seaweed suspended in gasoline. Infused with chamomile, organic herbs and oils- he purchased in bulk. The bottles would be clear plastic. Chunks of Mother Nature floating around in some sort of "colloidal suspension" - that was from the label. It mostly looked like designer vomit. Bath time was a big event for him. Although he usually had these extravaganzas at the worst possible time, like when I needed to pee or had guests. Sometimes if he was feeling really whacked he came out naked and impersonated a really dumb girl with his dick tucked between (and behind) his legs. Usually he did that when I was having a big party. It sorted out the fun people from the never-to-be-invited-agains.

While I dried myself from the shower I thought of all the people who had been in that bathroom doing that same thing. Underneath, in some hyperspace those memories remained ready to pop out if you could tune an arcing microwave oven to their frequency- or something. I don't get too into bringing all that to the surface or I start to lose faith in everything and get really depressed. And that is boring. I stared at the shiny new video camera. It was like a de-winged dragonfly smothered on the bed.

"OK, Vienna- can I come?"

"Naw baby, it's gonna be boring and I am sure you'd prefer spending some money and they have a Miu Miu store for boys here or at least they used too."

"Fine." I think her faith in my shopping was a bit strong.

Solange left for Vienna. She left me two thousand Euros plus food money and the hotel room was paid for on an account of hers. I had yet to do anything but try to fit into some clothes. I had become a professional space taker-upper. I would be stupid to complain.

I spent the first few days without Solange wandering around Paris. I bought a new backpack at the Esprit store and then wasted a lot of time trying to avoid the temptation of filling it with expensive things with Solange's money.

I had lunch at Georges on top of the Centre Pompidou. Really Starked-out and cold but there was a really cute waiter that worked there who I had seen on my last trip to Paris. Lo and behold he still worked there because there he was taking my order for vegan-ish sushi. The view was nice (of him and the city) and I could see the Sacre Coeur which I had previously sworn never to visit, simply on a whim. A rather vehement whim, but a whim just the same. I don't know why- I guess it was one of my anti-tourist genes getting the best of me because I am sure I would like it. All white and old, melting like some frozen cum mausoleum in the sun. Oh well…

Sexy waiter guy was mumbling a bit in English to me as he slipped the dish of sushi on the table.

"I'm sorry- what did you say?"

"I was saying that if you would like to come to a party then I would like to invite you." His green eyes, black hair and his French "I'll take over the world" nose--not to mention his accent--cut through the distance between us like a shark. What is it with me and waiters? And sharks for that matter? Something about me makes people at ease. Like they can just come up and be my friend. Am I that see-through?

So I said the only French word I knew for sure would not give the wrong impression.

"Oui."

I think I have managed to elevate the deciphering of party directions written on the back of a match book into an art form. The scrawl that "Waiter Guy" (turned simply Guy) penned on the back of mine was almost Hebrew in character density. The only way I knew I was at the right place was that he was there too- although either of us could have made a mistake in getting there anyway.

18ième Arrondissement. Smoking. Someone in love with an *Oriental Garden* double cd of Middle Eastern Muzak. Slight dub reggae shuffle with a hit of Arabic wailing. Incense that was what sandalwood was suppose to smell like. The kind that never finds itself imported to a Wholefoods Market near you. A bunch of tan to brown French slash African guys who had no problem speaking about 5 languages lay on sofas that I am sure Solange would have called 'divans.' Gauzy draperies and candles were strewn about like a harem. The guys were wearing little more than cotton sheets. Thankfully, no eunuchs in sight.

Guy was all hot to trot that I had shown up. Which was weird because he was way cuter than me. Maybe once again my American-ness was working in some mystical way. Or they were planning on kidnapping me. Whatever. I was bored.

"Hello Johnny these are some of my more fun friends."

"Hi." I waved around the room and there was a localized murmur of salutations. A girl with a nose ring, long black hyper light-refracting hair and eyes that made you all religious got up and motioned towards me. It made me feel like I was at a restaurant/temple.

"You like a drink?"

"Yeah that would be great."

She sashayed away towards the cooler- it was dark and veiled- I couldn't see a fridge. I couldn't really tell. I was so nervous that I was relieved to see that the beer she was holding was an unopened bottle. My mother loved to regale me with stories of dosed party drinks. Fun.

Although she looked like an Ariadne or a Scheherazade, psycho doe-eyed girl's name was Cindy. I didn't know what her accent was though, kinda carmelly, nasal, sexy and cruel sounding. She was the anti-Amelie, looking to stick all her sharp edges into someone.

"Have you heard of this thing called 'disco dumping?"

Her eyes were all wild with crazy magnetisms, but the way she talked was totally out of sync- like she was being poorly dubbed.

"I thought it was a New York City thing, Guy said you were from New York City."

"Um yeah, I mean no, I'm from Boston."

"Do you say New York City or NYC? I think NYC sounds cooler." Cindy was drunk or high. And I think she was faking her whole thing- she could have been from Idaho for all I knew.

Guy took the beer from her hand and gave it to me. It still had a crust of ice on it from the cooler and made my fingers freeze.

"Let's go out on the terrace Jon-Jon." Guy was into nicknames. I felt like a brand new American toy. "Cindy is a bit of a messy tonight."

I was led out to a terrace that abutted the adjoining building so thoroughly that there was only a vertical view of the sky. It graciously filled with the stars that Guy required to make his move on me. I set the bottle of beer down and wiped my wet cold hands against the back of my pants. Classy.

"It's beautiful huh? Paris. I always wanted to be a poet so I would know what to say about it." Oh brother.

"Yeah- it's one of my favorite places." Even though I was facing a brick wall. Someone put on Samia Farrah. She ran in liquid Nutrasweet rivulets out to the terrace. I loved that cd.

"You have been here before?"

"Yeah, I've even been to Georges before, last year. I even remember you."

"You're good with faces huh?" Guy smiled but he seemed a little off-put, as if my attempted compliment misfired. He seemed preoccupied now that I would finger him for a bank robbery or something instead of just fingering him.

"My memory isn't <u>that</u> good, I just remembered you."

"Oh."

He got closer to me- hand on mine, sizable hard-on pressed to my right thigh.

A big boy popped his head out of the apartment. He was sexy in a Yeti kind of way. He shouted at Guy en francais.

"Cindy's boyfriend, Guillaume. He is a bit crazy."

Guillaume seemed as close to breathing fire on me as anybody ever had.

"He doesn't understand English- don't need to worry."

Guillaume shouted a bit more. He bored holes in Guy with his wacky space-shot eyes.

"Please excuse me, I have to talk with him. I'll only be seconds." He smiled crookedly, obviously embarrassed, pushed his boner down in his pants and followed Guillaume inside.

I nodded and thought about leaving. I figured I could make the party a bit more private and wheel Guy back to my hotel room. He came back a bit more embarrassed.

"Cindy has done that thing she was talking about."

"Sorry, what?"

"This disco dumping, she has dumped and now she's sliding around in there. Guillaume is threatening to kill her and all his boyfriends have left. It smells terrible. Fucking bisexuels"

"She does 'E'?"

"She does 'E' if 'E' stands for everything." Guy looked a little like a favorite photo of mine taken by Man Ray – surrealist traitor Philippe Soupault, shirtless, in a bowler hat and umbrella- but he had neither. And faggots make better poets anyway.

"Want to leave? I have a hotel room."

Guy's cock was what Kevin would call 'war-torn.' It was like weirdly circumcised or something. He let me fuck him against the mirrored wall of the hotel bathroom. The condom was translucent green so it looked like I was shoving a big frog suffering from amelia up his ass. And that, of course, made me think of all the mutant frogs that these middle school kids had found at a pond on the Cape last summer which then led to thoughts of global warming and the deadly radiation fucking up all the life forms on earth. Malformed frogs were documented in almost all fifty states, in almost forty species of frogs and almost twenty species of toads, with deformities running as high as sixty percent. If all the frogs died the planet would be overrun by insects. Voracious giant insects. In essence, I had suddenly found myself having sex in one of Solange's sci-fi horror films.

Guy was speaking French softly like he was starring in some other, much more romantic, TV movie of the week. It was, however, raining outside like that scene in *Irma Vep* where Maggie Cheung steals the jewelry from the naked woman crying on the telephone. So it could have been much more awe-inspiring if I just stopped letting my mind wonder from Guy's ass. It was like another person. It had a personality completely disconnected from him. And Guy's twin was hungry. Ok, ok, sweaty too.

"I think your friend Cindy was mad that we left."

"She," moan, grunt "is not my friend, I know Guillaume."

"Oh." Slobber, groan. "She seemed really um, trashed."

"She's diabetic and a junkie I think. Harder." Pant.

Guy and I got along really well and even better when I woke up and he had already left without stealing anything. Later he called me and asked if I wanted to go to dinner some night. I said "oui" again.

Solange called.

"I was chased down an alley in Vienna by a bunch of school kids."

"What?"

"They were throwing rocks at me. They seemed to know who I was."

"It's from the horror films. They must really think you are a demon. Doesn't that happen all the time?"

"No."

"No what? You said people freak sometimes when they recognize you."

"It was because they had been sent to do it."

She must have snapped- she was being paranoid.

"Solange that is crazy. Who would send a bunch of kids to attack you." It sounded like something that would happen in *The Village of the Damned*. Maybe she had lost it. Too much fashion, too much style- the girl had gone wild. Too many papier mache zombie sores and green body paint in her past catching up with her all at once.

"I saw a guy motion towards me to some kids across the

street. They picked up some gravel and threw them at me. That was when I started to run, tried to get into a crowd and get lost."

"Did you get a cop?" I could picture her running in her impossible heels, stones hitting the ground around her like battleship gray hail.

"It happened so fast and it was over so quick. I didn't have a chance to even think about getting help." Now at this point I was more than a little pissed that she was wondering around Austria without me.

"Do you remember what the guy looked like? You should file a report."

"I just want to get the hell out of here. I'll call you when I have the exact arrival time." Click.

Amateur artist that she was, she faxed the hotel a little doodle of him for me with the words 'just killing time' written on it. The face was a little sad, actually- the face of someone who cares too much about things that can't be changed- someone who gets mad at gravity.

It reminded me of Candy's ex-boyfriend from college.

She used to tell me that she wanted myself and some of my less-than-nice friends to rape him. He was the one that beat her up and threw her from a moving car. She wanted him to be fully destroyed. Well, at least, sodomized. I always thought he would like it too much so maybe that was why I said no. "You are barking up the wrong tree if you think that will bring his spirits down."

"Yeah but you could take pictures." She retorted with a

smirk.

I guess she found someone else to do it because I heard about it in the paper later- after she had moved back to Texas or wherever. The article was bland but I filled in the details. He had been dosed at a party and woke with a really big piece of latex up his ass. He was lying in a puddle of piss on cold concrete. The concrete basement floor of a new house. He couldn't take the thing out of his butt because his hands were taped but I don't think he felt that much discomfort actually. He did not know if all the spooge on his chest and legs was his or someone else's.

Guy called me. He wanted to have that dinner. He mentioned that his sanity-challenged friends might tag along. I almost said no, but I had nothing else to do. The place was a hangout of a kind for his entire crowd.

I copied the restaurant address down at Guy's request and followed the directions from a website map of Paris. I wasn't really familiar with that part of the city.

It was a weird casual place, like a sarcastic backhanded compliment to American comfort food. I had been waiting for Guy for about fifteen minutes when I decided to just get a table. A woman in her thirties and a child sat on my right, staring blankly at their steamy entrees. The little girl had on a little white dress with tiny cats on it. She had been attempting to write her name with a Sharpie on her sneakers. Patrizia. She drew the word slowly over and over on the white plastic soles. Both of them had sat with their backs to the window. The window was floor to ceiling. This Querelle-ish guy gave me a cute smile. Then he kept bringing himself to my attention with weird coughs and flourishes. He was sitting alone too. I think he was going to introduce himself or say something to me. But my favorite young couple interrupted all that normal fun flirtation stuff. Or more to the point, my "luck" was catching up to me in France. It took me a while to remember where I had seen them before- in fact, it took the pictures in the newspaper the next day for me to really realize that these two were Guy's friends, Guillaume and that lullaby league member, Cindy.

They seemed a bit out of place. A bit lost. They looked like they hadn't slept in a long time. I didn't even make a move to say hi or anything. I immediately felt the vibe they were giving off- like the rot of something left in the trash. I can only wonder what that says about me if I am tuning into their wavelength. They started screaming at each other and then they got quiet. Guillaume had really perfected his Yeti-in-heat-defending-his-mate vocal delivery. A few people left the dining room. Violence boiled up. I could feel time begin to slow down and shred. It was a familiar kind of feeling. I wasn't even slightly surprised when Guillaume pulled out the gun.

With a single sharp intake of breath my world fell away. The tasty smells of the kitchen scorched into the stench of gunshot and burning. A chunk of wall fell. It was like one of those cartoons where all the little woodland animals get thrown into the air after an explosion and end up in a tangled bunch when they hit the ground. I stumbled into Querelle- actually he stumbled into me. He spun and flipped beyond my grasp like a bad ballerina. He hit the ground. I was on the floor now too. I couldn't help but stifle a little laugh and smile- not at him- I just never get to finish a meal in a restaurant.

I hunched over and looked into the eyes of that Querelle. Why was I always destined to meet waiters and sailor stand-ins? Why was I getting stuck in gunfights? I wanted to yell at him, ask him. His lips were bright red with blood, the color of cheap lipstick. He looked like he would like a kiss.

But the blood was on his lips.

"I'd like to kiss you." I whispered. "But the blood."

"Je sais." He nodded in a kind of involuntary way, as if he expected me to say that. I realized he was bleeding because he had bit his lip. I grabbed his hand and he forced a smile that swelled over the top of his pain.

I had to move my legs slowly from under him to keep them from falling asleep. Cindy had stopped screaming and pulled the gun from her boyfriend's hand.

She turned it first on him. Guillaume screamed something and she popped his head off with a click on the trigger. Of course he looked right at me just before this. My heart punched flat against my ribcage like the kids tesseracting to a two dimensional planet in *A Wrinkle in Time*. I couldn't breath. Or I was holding my breath.

Cindy's trigger finger was cut and it looked like she had caused some pain when she pulled it, cracking the first tentative scabby clot. Her face was a zero. She was defeated. She was also a lot skankier looking in daylight. Dark roots and a bit of junkie sallow to her complexion. I had no idea what moved her to this final scene in her life. Only that she had pretty much decided that she required a sizable audience for it. Guillaume lay dead in a pile of clothes and yeti chunks. His hair was wet and black and his eyes have gone shark-like. He had failed his final Quentin Tarantino audition.

Cindy let off a few more bullets randomly into the air like some deadly female ejaculation. Then she squeezed off a pop-pop from under her chin so the bullet passed through the middle of her head- perfectly-as if she had studied suicide in school and passed all the tests. Querelle grasped my arm more tightly when the gun went off for the fifth and final time.

Dull plops. Heavy stones in a deep pool. Cindy's crazy drug-pickled brains (eraser gray with blood like red jokes) flew against the wall and slid obscenely down, drip-drip-dripping now on the mess that was the wait station. The smell was strong: cooked white skin gone bad. The open windows brought more everyday smells from the street but these were like remember-when's for all the people prostrate under the tables. Valuable and faraway.

The front window had shattered easily from the impact of one of Cindy's bullets. One struck deep in the molding over the door frame I had come through. I couldn't figure out what she was aiming at. Maybe at Guy, he was really late. Or the whole world. Cindy, you needed a bigger gun.

I think I was in shock. I get funnier when I am in shock. I think.

The floor was alternating blocks of black and red. Querelle was pressed to a black tile, giving it the impression that the red tiles had melted onto his black tile and his black hair. He was talking a little -a bit of a monologue. Not the kind of thing that one would rehearse I suppose. Although he was making every attempt at getting the syllables to match how his lips were trying to move.

The weird blue-green birds on the tablecloths turned out to be dragonflies. I could see the design more clearly now – a portion of the table from the front of the room had been hurled to the back and rested a few feet from my head.

I sometimes think that if I open my eyes wide enough (figuratively of course) I'll see how big this whole existence is. I get the feeling sometimes, hard to describe. Like when you hear a song with a really beautiful string arrangement on it? And it makes the hair on the back of your neck stand up - I sometimes get that feeling just by looking at the city streets or the trees or the sky. Strange huh? Or it's just me getting old and thoughtful. I hate when that happens. The floor is even wetter after my little blackout, like I forgot to die.

Death abruptly reminds us that no matter how everyday our life can seem, no matter how many simple things crowd around us looking to be taken for granted in that comfortable haze of mundane numbness- no matter that we pretend and love and lie and sleep and eat and get married or cheat- no matter- the mystery of death always flits behind it all. No matter that we can watch some dumbass wannabe W.A.S.P. on television make 16 place mats from old vinyl siding or tell us how simple pleasures are good things. We are still going to be forced to see darkness.

In this I can feel the strangest thing about life. If we could only see its preciousness we would be free, but to do so we come face to face with our end and that is where the shuddering begins. People turn away from the Emily Dickinson special effects of it. They spin their heads away and try to pretend that this bland TV Guide they are living will continue forever.

The boredom of it almost works. The effort of it is almost enough.

It isn't that we don't try hard enough. There is so much stale 'ordinary' around for us to trip on. The dust of life. The way people make or buy accessories for their accessories. Purchasing small tools or seeing a movie or trying to lose weight. The filling up of time with common place- it works for a little while, whether that little while is a week or a life. But somewhere it fails and the mirror is removed and the real life comes in, and that real life is only revealed in a final breath. A final sigh. One last look at the sky and then a slow darkness that shutters down gradually, building to an endless fall.

I'm not going to let anyone close my eyes. I want to die with them closed. I want a little undertaker art and that's it. No careful hands need to cover my skin with expensive grave clothes. I want to go into the fire headfirst. No whining, cremate me- corpses don't panic. It was good enough for my cat- its good enough for me.

I'm standing there in my fantasy with gun in hand to free them from the everyday- almost like Cindy or a god. Almost a god or a devil and as silent as one too.

It's weird but I always think about sex when I think I am about to die. Maybe it's a way to deal with my fear. Who knows?

Anyway Querelle was staring at my hand. I reached across the noodle-strewn space between us and touched him again.

The smell of burnt everything was in the air. Time wobbled like a top about to stop spinning. The windows were gone and the breeze that came through their empty jagged frames was hot and dirty. People had dumped their umbrellas in a clump by the doorway- wet dead blackbirds electrocuted in the rain. The blood only underscored the awkward jumble. A crumbled umbrella is such a weird shape.

I remembered Candy's broken umbrella a few hundred New Year's Eve's ago. Once she broke up with the mortician and got to the big city she changed her hair, her whole look really. She used to fuck so much and with so many guys it was like she didn't wear clothes- she wore people. Lots of rich people. Designer people. I was always hiding her from some guy she had stood up. She would wash my kitchen floor on her hands and knees and talk about how this guy wanted to kill her. A lot of girls washed my kitchen floor as a way to kill time back then. I never understood it. Some guy had broken Candy's umbrella. He stabbed her with one of the pieces that held the fabric up. Not very deeply and she didn't feel it because she had been very high at the time. Later it upset her a lot. Her uncle had the guy killed. At least she said that- a lot. She took too much Sudafed to get high when she couldn't get a fix. It fucked her thyroid up. That's when she was rumored to have moved back to Texas.

The sounds of a car became evident and then those too were slowly removed from the immediate scene. I felt like I had somehow been dropped into a painting. Nothing moved. All the colors were bright, even the grays. No sound. Except the frying pans that had been abandoned. The smell of burning meat and oily smoke wafted into the dining area from the kitchen. The little girl slow-motion struggled to get out from under the table and her mother. She still had the Sharpie. It loyally drew a jagged line as she dragged it across the floor in her bloody hand. Broken glass gave her a shiny tiara-like halo encrusted with ruby and diamonds. Somehow her mother was also alive. They hugged on the floor. Sirens began, like the signal for an intermission.

I had, of course, peed my pants.

"I think it's over." The little girl said in French- in that kind of French child voice that always makes me mad that I can't speak French as well as a child. Her mother looked like she had shit her pants. She was clutching some bread that she had put to her mouth. The butter was half on her bottom lip and a bit on the collar of her orange shirt. It had already begun to moat grease around its edges. She'd never get that stain out now.

The sirens got closer and redder.

I changed my mind on whether to move. I just lay there. Querelle was quiet. He had stopped moving- or trying to move. I was just stroking his hair a bit as if I had fallen in love.

Smoke was coming from an ashtray. A cigarette was silently whining for attention. It would take about fifteen minutes before one of the uninjured waiters would feel safe enough to snuff out the cigarette, which is licking the tablecloth into a ring of red. Would every one of us have just left it burning like that if the woman had not stopped herself? Would we all have died of smoke inhalation while waiting for the woman to open fire on us? Weird thoughts, weird afternoon…

I felt my wallet in my pants pocket. It was pushing on my

leg and it felt like a hot rock. Bleeding a little. When Cindy had shot the waiter's station a lot of the place settings (dishes, forks, tea cups) were thrown into the air and a lot of glass came down on everyone. I must have a bit of glass in my leg. In fact, that was why we all had wounds. The stray bullets hadn't touched anyone.

I must have a small piece of glass in my leg. Again. In my leg. I touched Querelle to see if he was breathing. He groaned. He was alive.

It took forever for the ambulance to get there.

The paramedics and the police were shouting. It cracked our silence like an intrusion. Querelle was drooling onto my lap and I imagined it running into my pocket, filling up my wallet. He coughed. There was no glass in my leg. I was not bleeding.

The light was getting filtered through smoke.

The department store across the street has emptied its customers onto the sidewalks to gawk.

It took them a long time to help me up. I made statements to the police awkwardly trying some French. They looked at my passport. Thank god I am really paranoid and carry it around.

"There's nothing to worry about. What is your hotel? You will want to be around Paris to answer questions, if we have any."

Just like what they say to Audrey in Charade.

"Will you see that you friend gets home safely?" They motioned to Querelle. The police guy was trying to warm up and be more human.

"Yes, I just have to figure out where home is for him. Can I have my passport back?"

It's my only picture ID. The police didn't seem to listen to me but I think that it was that weird look that cops get when they listen to you talk about things they need to hear. They seem to be filtering the emotion out of your presentation- sifting the bullshit and fear for the facts they need. Almost always in these situations they don't look you in the eye. They stare hard and cold off into space, like doctors. Movies never get cops right. Of course- they could have been having a hard time with my English and pathetic French speaking skills. They handed back my passport.

After the paramedics where sure I had no serious injuries they offered to get me a cab but I said no. I left with Querelle. I wanted to walk. I think I was pretending that nothing had happened.

The light was gone, the day was skidding to an end.

As the police taped up the place, and people murmured how this never happens in Paris, the rain fell and the streets shone. The two ambulances pushed off from the sidewalk into the slow traffic like lazy boats. Stars came out. The sky revolved slowly. They were the same stars from last night, even though tonight they seemed restarted. My grandfather showed me all the constellations when I was a kid. He had navigated a bomber in World War 2 by the stars. He explained to me how they were some of the only things he still trusted in the world. Although some are no longer on fire, their hot hearts have long since folded into the infinite creases, collapsing onto themselves, but still invisibly tugging on the vast cathedral roofs of space.

I felt like I was going a little crazy. I've been a certain way so long that I think I have lost some important adaptation tool in my personality first aid kit. Or perhaps that being immune to love so long a weird strain of it has punctured my resistance and I have no ready defense against its onslaught. Whatever the case, I felt surreal. People in my everyday long ago life had lost their meaning and their importance. I kept wondering when I fell off the world.

I had reached a point there and then where the problem I was struggling with suddenly revealed all its parts. I could sit back and look at it, almost like a map or a graph. The point was to visualize it as something harmless, like a flower and not dangerous, like a razor blade. Then I could pull the petals off it slowly and kiss it all goodbye- at least until the next time. It does get better then, if I force myself to remember that there is always a next time and that the bad moments are all getting lost in the past as they occur. So much for the present – it's gone.

But Solange was part of the present and she was more than what she was saying. She had this whole other dimension that I couldn't see. As if she had all this extra ultraviolet spectrum of ulterior motives that I had no clue about. All her history surrounded her like some weird pheromone that I was unable to smell.

Fischerspooner were trying to have a hit in France. Good luck.

Although I was beginning to feel like I was the reason all this crazy mayhem occurred. Somehow my being at a certain spot created a void or a black hole that sucked violent people and situations towards me. And it followed that if I was the reason maybe I could control it better. Like a superhero. Or I could check myself into a clinic and talk to someone for a long time.

Guy had never showed up at the restaurant. I never heard from him again. I bet he knew that Guillaume and Cindy were planning a little dinner theater and decided to opt out. I just wish he had R.S.V.P.'d me and saved me the trouble. Literally. Jerk.

Querelle, whose name was Alain, I decided to call Al because he didn't look like one and I didn't think he would like it. His dark hair is really not that dark once it dried. He spoke slowly in English. I pretended not to understand him so I can hear his voice test the syllables. He was cute. Not overwhelmingly so, but cute just the same.

His flat was great. High ceilings, fancy plaster- big framed prints of things like Les Rita Mitsouko's *The No Comprendo* album cover, all that remained of French New Wave glory. It was like a bit of the sexy Euro cool 80's died here and a shrine got erected.

Alain read really silly American novels from the 80's about gay serial killers and alienated Gen X coke whores from Los Angeles. Books that talked about punk rock being something that had rules or dogmas involved with it. Books that nailed coffin covers down on themselves. I told him that anyone who doesn't get paid to go on killing sprees is an idiot.

"Anyone who writes a book about serial killers is too boring to be a pervert."

He agrees but doesn't shuffle any books from his bookcases on my account. They just sit there underlining our lack of similarities. And the fact that Solange had turned my life into a sideshow. But it was nice to be with him. He was normal and kind. And a bit rich.

"Why are you in Paris, Johnny-Jon."

I was destined to have my name warped by French guys.

"I am working on a restaurant show for TV with this actress/hostess, Solange. She's going to call me in a few days when she returns to Paris." I suddenly couldn't wait to see her. Now my weird violent current events at least could compete with her alley-stoning fiesta. Maybe that was a bad thing to be aiming for but it felt ok then. The alley thing was beginning to bug me a bit. Even after the shoot out in "le corral."

"And when she gets here, could you not tell her about this whole shootout thing? I don't really want to make a big deal out of it."

"Why? You just don't want to tell her?"

"Well she brought me here and then she split for some business meeting and I don't want her to think it was her fault or that I can't handle things. I don't want to be thought of as accident prone."

"So then, how did we meet? What will you say to her

about how we met?"

"I don't know. How do any guys meet anyway? At a bar is fine."

"Okay but I don't like to lie."

"Okay, then just nod. I will lie."

He seemed a little confused. Confusion looked good on him. His eyes got all watery and half desperate, almost like he was about to cum but didn't want to just yet and was trying to resist it.

"Did you save my life? I can't remember what happened very well."

"No I didn't save you. We just fell on top of each other when we were scrambling to avoid Cindy."

"Cindy?"

"Yeah that was her name."

"How do you know?"

"I had met her before."

That wide-eyed look that translates in any culture as "Who the hell are you?" came over Alain.

"She was at a party that I went to. One of her friends invited me and then he wanted to take me to dinner at a place that his crowd always goes too. He didn't show up but his friends did."

"That is crazy. You just met her the other day?"

"A few days ago. I figured she was pretty fucked up when I met her. If I had known she was going to be at the restaurant I wouldn't have gone."

"And you would never have met me." Alain got that watery eye look again.

"This happens to me all the time." I joked, telling the truth. The best kind of communication. In French though, I couldn't tell what tense I was using.

"I am lucky." If being caught in a shootout is lucky. Alain had something in his eye now for real and he brushed it away slowly, absently.

"I still have restaurant in my eyes. I lost my cell phone there too."

"They're like cockroaches- they always survive. It had probably slid under a table or the bar."

"Or someone had stepped on it." He looked sexy, disheveled and just-in-from-combat.

Sometimes good things do happen. But I've found that I can't wait for them. That's an old lie. The only thing that comes to those who wait is age.

I didn't wait for Alain to come in for a landing kiss. I turned him around in the kitchen and made good on my mid-carnage promise. We ended up on the floor again. But in a good sweaty way.

We went to buy him a new phone the next day. He picked a Nokia- shiny blue like a rain forest frog. Alain's apartment smelled really familiar. The mornings were beautifully slow.

I spent way too much time on the phone and Alain paced a lot trying to understand my English. I think I was feeling mortal and frail.

I called my grandmother out of the blue. I was feeling mortal again from the recent events. She was surprised that I was in Paris. I had to reassure her that all the phones in the world were compatible.

She sounded so ancient, which of course is normal as she is about 800 years old. I could hear all kinds of things in her voice. Although she's only talked about the weather and her garden for as long as I've known her- I could tell she wasn't really thinking about any of that anymore, if she ever really did. It was a mask for all the things she couldn't say to me about what she was feeling. She used to kid about it when I was younger. Called it "the final curtain." She feels that curtain but on other people. I don't know if I could survive the way she has without granddad. But then I suppose I would have to have gotten married and had a wife or someone around for that to be a problem. See, even my problems have problems.

Of course, grandmother has great pieces of advice like

"At a certain age smoking is a necessity" and "Cancer can sometimes be welcomed with open arms." She wasn't openly suicidal but with little heartwarming chats like that you never can tell where you're going to find her. In the bathtub like an exploded maraschino cherry or as the incredibly flat woman on the sidewalk outside her apartment. I kidded about it but I didn't want her to do it and I certainly didn't want to be the one to find her.

During our uplifting little "talk" the call-waiting burped. It was Solange.

"I'm on Air France I'll arrive in Paris at 9:30 pm. The Viennese guys liked my ideas. They're in for a nice bunch of money. It was almost worth being stoned for. How have you been?"

"Great. I met a guy."

The rain didn't stop for about the next three days. The air was heavy with the smell of what the wet had shaken loose- all the old stuff sticking to Paris. My mouth slack, hoping to catch a few drops. It had a rusty taste- like water from an ancient bathtub. Solange and I stood in it on Al's little balcony.

"At night I used to get so lost here. We'd come into town to do a runway thing modeling blue furs for Claude Montana or something equally whack." She was wearing a turquoise YSL modernized gypsy dress. I usually hate turquoise. It's a cheap color. But it was also quite see-through so the color was muddled to startling effect with Solange's skin. Of course, she was totally over-dressed. Wardrobe-wise I figured she lived in a world where gardening didn't exist. "So we'd do a show for Giacomo's agency and then we'd all run wild through the streets. The eighties fucking rocked." Okay, Fallon.

The sky was that dark blue Crayola with a billion stars sticking their cold bright pinheads down at us. We walked for a little bit to get the night settled in our heads, talking about old movies as we watched the Seine recycle its own romance in the distance.

I ordered pizza and Solange described the town of Pavia, Italy to Alain, a place she hoped to shoot a show in, while we listened to *Voices of Drum and Bass, Volume 1.* I had rescued it from the mess of the bag I had brought with me to the restaurant. It only skipped on the first track.

"It's small, old. Has an amazing pizza place that I want to do a show on. Quaint but with great shops. My friend Ruggero retired there." She sipped a bit of wine. She did everything slow motion when she talked. It seemed to keep the emphasis on her lips. "Well he didn't retire- he just found a rich doctor and moved his whole family up there. All ten of them, Sicilian. I can only imagine what they think of that arrangement. And the weather just isn't the same. He gave up this house in Sicily that was amazing. At night, you could see lights across the water, lights in Africa." She swayed and nodded a little bit to Juju's "Evolution Revolution."

Alain was fussing with the sofa. He'd pulled the chenille cover off it and was tugging.

"I know it pulls out. I just have to find the lever."

The two of them started tugging on the couch. It reminded me of people trying to unbeach a pilot whale.

At least the whole Solange thing didn't seem to tense Alain up and it led to some more wine and kissing. He liked when I talked to him as if I understood everything he was saying. When the rain did stop, the sky flexed through the clouds- with a full moon over the city like a big bald head haloed through the silver mist.

I was a bit calmer now and I almost forgave her for the whole abrupt leave-me in Paris thing. Almost. Until I found a handgun in one of her bags. Not that I should have been looking in her stuff but she asked me to move it into the room Alain had for her and I couldn't help but feel it in the bag. Or something that felt and weighed like a gun. So I looked, yup a gun.

He hates that I call him Al. I figured.

I didn't say anything to Solange about finding a gun in her bag. I don't know why. Maybe I just couldn't take getting the whole truth and nothing but just now. I left it where it was, but I took note of what bag it had been in.

I couldn't sleep that night. It was like all the stars above me were tied to little strings that were waving in the night, creeping down to attach themselves to individual brain cells through my scalp. Kinda a Bjork image I know but I was feeling like I was guilty of something. Something that I didn't even know if there was a name for it. And people get so wrapped up in language here to. Maybe I should have gone to sleep but I couldn't get my head to shut off. I couldn't even let go of my breathing. When I get like that I have to walk the streets. Even if the streets aren't somewhere I am familiar with.

Walking around alone at night in Paris isn't so bad as long as you don't go to anywhere too far out.

I felt a bit on edge. The calm that had gotten a hold of me the past few nights there was wearing off. Solange wanted us to be leaving soon. I was trying to make bets with myself to see when she would give that signal. She hadn't told me what she was planning to do or when she was planning for us to start to work. I almost didn't want to know. The idea of going to Italy was enough though.

Alain put on this old compilation that had Chic's 'Good

Times' on it. The irony of it made me feel like I was in a Quentin Tarantino film. Never a good sign. Alain had started to show some cracks. He rarely went out anymore. He avoided restaurants and started cooking at home.

I wish it was warmer here but the summer is almost over and the cold metal feel in the air was giving me bumps all over my skin. Skin crickets like Kevin used to say. Oh well... another night picking up the plot of some dinner with survivors. I yawned like a cat.

The atmosphere had fallen a bit with Alain. He left to buy some cigarettes and I realized that I hadn't realized he smoked. His hair caught the light from the hallway as he left the flat but it shadowed his face so he'd gotten a bit of a weird profile but no features. A scene out of *The Exorcist* or something. I went into the compact kitchen and got some water. The water hasn't been put in the fridge so it was a bit warm. Warm and bubbly. Not my favorite.

The sky was torched overhead. All grays and reds and streaks of blue higher up. The CD player was making Sade cry. I was turning to face the wall these days. I knew I had to calm down a bit or I was going to have to get a real day job and that would really suck. I was not ready for that kind of boredom just yet. I realized that Alain's apartment smelled like cats. That is what the familiar smell is and it made me think of my cat and my apartment in Boston. My brother was supposed to be taking care of her, I imagined that he would be giving too much cheap canned cat food. I'd come home to a fat lazy rug of a cat.

Outside the pastel lights were melting in the fog. I curled up on a couch by the window. There were students down below making young noises. I realized the bag of faux French M and M's I was eating had 500 calories in it. I was appalled at my body now. I've got to do something about that.

Solange's stuff was gone. I think she had left when I was out getting some groceries. She called later

"Hey baby, I am back at the hotel. I wanted to give you some space with that cutie. And you know I am a slave for hotel housekeeping services. I have room 48. We should start thinking about Italy! Ciao bello."

Again, not even a shred of anything in her voice to say "yeah my behavior is erratic and weird." Maybe she was off some medication. At least she was still in the same city as me.

Alain went out late with friends that night to the Queen. I saw in the paper that the restaurant had been boarded up after the suicide couple. They were in love. The papers all referred to a long letter that the Cindy's mother received in the mail about how in love they were and that they were going to have the best honeymoon in heaven, just like heaven. A lot of space shot hippy stuff, which is funny because they didn't strike me as particularly new age, just angry and self-destructive.

My back was killing me. I have to have someone massage it soon or I will not be able to move. There was a hole in it- a tight pull. It was better now but it would come back and I would be in agony. I had to stop eating all this garbage.

Seeing America on the news here was like a giant commercial for something that didn't exist. I hadn't even noticed how faraway it seemed to me here. Maybe thinking about my cat made me a little homesick.

I fell asleep and dreamt that Solange and I were at the top of the Statue of Liberty. We were in the torch and when we looked down it was like the view from an airplane- impossibly high up. We tried to get down because I was scared of heights but the stairwell was filled with logs of wood so we had to dig and lift our way down and out. It ended before we could leave. I think it means I am constipated. Or America is constipated. Probably both.

There was a turning point coming. I could feel it. Tonight at dinner I felt like a great wave of violence was coalescing in me and then Alain beat it out of me. My ass was still red.

We'd fallen off the bed and gotten all this lubricant on the floor and kept sliding around. His cock was bent almost at a right angle. When I felt it my first thought was, can I live my life married to a cock this crooked? Nice wedding vows. He gave blow jobs like you were plugging into a heaven receptacle. And the best thing was that he spoke French the whole time and I could tell it was really dirty French. Sometimes just the way a word is delivered is enough to let you in on the plot, no need to really understand.

I felt a little woozy too. Something in the water, or in the food. All fucked out. It almost felt like I was summoning the violence like a demon or something.

2.5 billion clichés, starting with the caterpillar in the cocoon becoming a beautiful butterfly, screech through my head. "We're going to Italy to start filming. Aren't you excited?"

"Yes, finally."

"I know it's been a strange time to get adjusted to me but it's better than a cubicle right?"

"Definitely." If you erase the shootout in my head it was perfect.

It's late. I feel like I have been arriving at this moment for a long time but only now do I have all the right ideas and clues ironed out, pinned down, starched and color coded. Tagged. Ready. For what? War? Planting a tree? Who knows. All that I know is that in the end, I'll get paid. That's what Solange says.

The hole in the ozone layer has split into two. They are drifting up in the globe. Or so the newscaster said in French. My head was spinning with prophecies- trying to decide if this pitifully written CNN report heralded the dawn of some Happy Meal Antichrist.

"I want you to come to my place tonight."

Alain was having people over for dinner. He invited me but I can't do French food and French conversations right now plus I was packing for Italy. Too much divided attentions. My French was worse than my 11th grade French teacher, Madame Plettner, who taught an entire semester of French talking out of the side of her mouth because of her Bell's palsy. It was ridiculous. And I am a bit scared that my accent has been effected by her weird pronunciations.

"I am going to stay at the hotel. I have to get ready and pack up for Italy. At least, that was Solange is saying."

He soothed me with a lot of love-you's and adjectives that sound really sexy and yet utilitarian – like the truth almost. I stared at the screensaver on my laptop as he slurred. I realized this Frenchman is drunk.

"What kind of dinner party are you throwing if you are drunk?"

"The kind where after dinner you have to take off your clothes."

This sounds vaguely stupid and I begin to slide my finger to the End button on the cell phone. But then Alain blurted out:

"There was a man who was looking for Solange and you. I don't know how he knew you were here. I said you left me and I didn't know where you were. Which wasn't a lie, by the way." Those sentences were first in French which I forced him to repeat three times in English until he got all the words right. A Solange stalker.

"What did he look like?"

"Older, bad skin. "

I figured it was one of her old friends she had mentioned she had in Paris, but it was weird that he was going around to Alain's. Unless she had mentioned that she was staying there.

I told Alain I would come back from Italy soon to see him. I think he told me to fuck off or something to the equivalent, which I couldn't understand. At that moment I was so nervous I didn't realize that Alain was upset that I was leaving. Really upset.

He was scared to leave the apartment now. I guess he was having some sort of post traumatic effect from the shooting. I was doing my best to ignore his emotions. Maybe I was suffering too.

My new insectoid cell phone stung me- it was my

parents. They've decided that they want to rent a house in Umbria or maybe Tuscany and they would really appreciate me picking one out etc.

"Maybe your friend from the Italian movies can help, Solange?"

Oh Mom, you are the best...

The breeze was soft on my face and for a short moment there I forget where I am and why I am. Seldom do I let myself get so wrapped up in nostalgia- this year has been a weird drop in a really rusty bucket.

That lunar landing song was on the radio and it reminds me of Costes and that really stupid afternoon with anus model aging face woman. And then I laugh a little instead thinking that maybe she wasn't a model at all- just some old tart that hadn't even seen her glory days or even her expiration date go by. Crème brulee face.

My gum got stale. Like chewing a stiff tongue. The showers at this hotel are very lux. They make anyone feel like a very well paid movie star awaiting good news at Cannes. At least- that was the intention I think. It works for me.

My laptop had a little bloodstain on the lid. The screen part. I don't know how it got there. It's shaped like Ceylon. Triangular... I think some sort of tea comes from Ceylon. Blood. Actually I think Ceylon is Sri Lanka now.

Nights were coming over me like gray fog banks. I didn't see Alain before I left with Solange. I wanted to get away from the memory of how we met.

The first real 'job' she had lined up was to be in Italy. We flew Swissair to Malpensa. Plane lands. People get out like a magic show that's over. This is the kind of moment that Solange relishes in. She knows that the minute she walks through that door into customs that everyone will be looking at her. They won't be able to help themselves. And you know, it isn't in a bad way- she isn't a car crash- she is really stunning. She'll even drop something (a scarf or a set of car keys (someone else's))to give a more human fallible glow to her charm. Her gravitational pull is akin to Jupiter. Men will fall. There will be almost no hassle at the customs desk. She will slip in like water through a crack.

We took a cool shuttle train thing to Milan and then another smaller bus to Pavia. It was here that she had that old friend, Ruggero, a make-up artist from her "drama years." The 'drama years' was what she called her Italian film career. She also wanted me to meet another friend of hers who owned a small modeling agency in Milan that had represented her for a while in the late eighties. "A boutique" she said, winking. Giacomo was also involved in restaurants somehow as a partner and would make maybe an interesting person to interview but she glossed over that all with the fashion/model talk. I was really intrigued, I assured her.

Solange made introductions, and then slithered into the background. She was in a strange electro-clash fusion outfit-pink mixed with some weird snake skin leatherized plastic swishy skirt stuff.

"I'm picking out want-to-knows from the left-behinds in the living room, darling" She said over her shoulder with all this "I'm getting laid" gusto.

It was just at this point that I saw the real echo effect of Solange. It's like you see a person in a certain light for a while and form an opinion of them but then I saw her in the midst of this party and she was like an fiery Hindu goddess burning a path through the room. At that point you go "woah" as you see the real effect of someone on a room. Her personality or whatever you call it. Her aura was just radiating into the people and you could see the effect she was having on them. Maybe like a shielded isotope uncovered suddenly. It was all very subliminal and subconscious but she was on top of it all. I'm sure anyone there could have gone home with her if she had waved her hand in their direction. I know that sounds silly but she gave off this kind of Japanese beetle kill you in the corner of the backyard hormone attraction vibe that was impossible to ignore. A bug zapper of love, if you will.

Cue Ruggero.

"Ciao Johnooooo! Solange has told me so much about

you. So much and it is all mostly good of you as well!"

Outside, my head nodded and my face smiled. Inside I made extensive notes about lighting and atmosphere. It was a great place for shooting an interview.

Ruggero was what Dolce and Gabbana had in mind whenever they designed a bold leopard and lemon printed something that most can't ever imagine wearing. Not only was his bedroom (which he shared with the solemn, graying doctor, Marco) covered in a safari's worth of animal print- it was filled with enough fur to suffocate a kindergarten. In many ways it resembled the interior of Barbarella's space ship sans the likelihood of Jane Fonda- or any woman for that matter, reclining in it- nude or otherwise.

He had decorated the living room in a strange dark opium den kind of way. The hallways felt like they were on a luxury liner below decks. The place was packed with slicked haired brown-eyed babes lounging around looking for places to spray paint their personalities. Bebel Gilberto was singing from artfully disguised speakers all over the flat. Then someone put in Pino Daniele, which is the Italian equivalent of a lot of music I called 'panty-peeler.'

The flat was actually the penthouse and there was an authoritative view of the center of Pavia, away to the left was a great bit of trees with the river and a few graceless asymmetrical apartment buildings along it. The center of the town was beautifully plugged with a fat crusty heel of bread Duomo.

I was having a headache crisis and Ruggero was divvying out the aspirin from a tiny ivory pill case in the kitchen. Giacomo arrived at that moment. His excuse was that he had gone to college with Ruggero.

"Ciao Giacomo- this is John."

"John, ciao!"

"Ciao Giacomo- how are you?"

Giacomo was a bit regal, almost like a haughty prince. His nose was evened out by his smile which was halogen bright but warmer. His eyes were deep and shining. He didn't look 47. I was in trouble. I could feel the trouble and it was starting in my chest and not my pants. The worst kind of trouble. I almost looked for Solange. I almost tried to get her to leave with me.

"How are you finding Italy?"

"Found it, love it. I feel I've been here before. My mother's family is from Italy."

"You must feel the Italian in your blood no?"

Giacomo stared at his lizardy green shoes, tapping the floor softly, then looked up directly into my eyes.

"Yeah I guess so." Accents can disarm even the cheesiest clichés.

He was concerned for how many aspirin I took, checked the milligrams on the bottle and barked at Ruggero about how to take aspirin. This was in Italian so I was not sure really what he barked. He turned to me, a bit stern. His lips were not unpleasantly thin. Strong lines of the chin and jaw.

"Where are your mother's parents from?"

"My grandmother's family is from Naples, but she was born in the USA. My grandfather was born in Rome." I thought, at least, that was what I had always been told. We had a huge grape arbor when I was little, so I assumed a lot.

"So you're southern!"

"Well, yeah- by the long way round."

"Good."

"Why?"

"The northerners have colder hearts."

I certainly was going to gain some experience on that blanket statement, I was sure. I don't think he understood what I was saying most of the time. Not that I had tried to explain myself anyway. I just acted crazy- my sixth sense was malfunctioning. My body language was not though.

I felt kinda light headed. He'd taken my feet out from under me like a blow job. Solange stood in the kitchen doorway.

"Hola Johnny." She had been doing a Carmen Maura impression for the throng, walking back and forth in the living room in her heels like a woman on the verge. "How is it going? Anything good?"

"Yeah, I think you already know."

"I think that you are right."

"So what's going on?"

"Isn't this place beautiful? Should I buy a place here? I like how handy it is to the city but still has a small town vibe."

"Sure, it would be beautiful."

"Then when you are living here in Milan with Giacomo I

can visit more"

"You're crazy."

"He really likes you. He sat in the living room just now talking about you."

"This is like grade school."

"A little, but with better food and nicer classrooms."

"Uh-huh."

Later, on Ruggero's terrace or roof – I couldn't figure out what to call it, Solange lay in the hammock swinging slowly back and forth. I would have gotten really sea sick but she seemed fine.

"Nice life." Solange draped herself lethargically over it.

"This is the life. Not my life," She whispered to me. "But a nice life." Then she started singing along with Pino.

There should be a word for infatuation that links lust and love more closely. I bet there is one in Italian. That feeling that you are in love but actually you are just completely sucked into someone's gravity well. Romantic yes, real no.

Pavia was not only home to Ruggero. It was home to Pizzeria Marechiaro in the Piazza Vittorio and the best pizza I have tasted so far. It was about to touch my (almost dripping) tongue. All pertinent taste buds began a vigil.

This was the last perfect moment of pure stupidity-bliss I would have in Italy. My internal, organic hard drive began recording the little barbs that Ruggero was tossing Giacomo.

"Giacomo next time you should meet Solange and John at the airport- surely you could spare the hour."

"I couldn't make the airport to meet them. My uncle fell and I had to make sure the restaurant opened…"

He began to elaborate the excuse, verbally unfurling a white flag of surrender to me that brought the idea of bed sheets to me.

My brain, wrenched from this pizza's White Witch Turkish Delight effect was now listening to notice the voice.

"…get someone to help him and he is very old and my mother…"

At Rugg's apartment I was too freaked out by the weird noir *Love Boat* feel of the place. Here it was easier to focus. His voice was 'nice.' As in "Nice to meet you- can we have sex on your terrace? You have a terrace don't you? With a voice like that you must have a terrace."

His nouns and verbs were simply vehicles for this melodious version of halfway decent English. Italian passed from Ruggero to Giacomo. I took this as plots and hidden motives-- as I do when anyone speaking a language I don't understand does so right in front of me. Who doesn't? OK maybe I was paranoid.

Solange just sat imperiously at the head of the table, staring at the busboys, practicing her Italian on them with a vague detached smile. She drank red wine and smoked cigarettes.

The voice in my head, (the voice that is constantly trying to take over full control of my fucking life) said: "Take notes." Of course, even with this kind of inoculation I was totally taken over and by surprise. There's no rubber for the heart.

"This pizza is of course, excellent. When you come to Milan you will have some great meals at my restaurant. Have you ever had a pizza like this?" Something about him was eminently detestable but it made the parts of him that were appealing even more so. A hate to love you that won out over the love to hate you.

I had never had a pizza like this. It was beyond good. It was thin crusted, barely sauced with Parmesan as the only cheese on it. It was one of the most heavenly things in the entire world. I also quickly picked up the reference to my 'future' presumed visit to Milan.

Giacomo was so proud of pizza- as if he had been responsible for it.

"This is probably the best pizza I have ever had."

"You have a very marketable smile."

"Huh?"

"Your smile, it's very commercial. I manage models. Solange once." He winked at Solange and she made a gesture at him that seemed to suggest he should shut up.

"And what could you sell with it?"

"A smile? A good smile sells food and furniture. Print ads. Not every model is on a runway for Gucci or Prada."

Just what I wanted to hear. I could sell sofas and grapefruit. A typical kind of story for me, I could be in a glamorous kind of profession like modeling but I would be hawking ravioli and desks.

"So I inspire domesticity?"

"Si and trust." He laughed. "A good smile says trust me."

His chin had a small bit of cheese on it.

I think he was scared to meet me- Solange can really hype someone up or maybe he had a weird sense of clairvoyance- but not enough to save him. He was so nervous- his laughter was all blood at the surface and sweat softened. It was the laugh of someone who wants to be loved at all costs- the kind of thing that gets guys mislabeled 'charming' when in fact they're ingenious. I am a sucker for that. It's a powerful spell- it gets past the highest defenses of someone like me.

We left my brain and Ruggero's little party behind. Solange said she would stay in Pavia. She'd call me later in Milan, where Giacomo lived in style.

The night opened inward and all the air from outside rushed to us, filled with all those pinpricked stars and amber night-light traffic stops.

The highway splashed all silvery-black around Giacomo's car. The rain left reflections of the other car headlights trailing on the windows, like the cover of a old jazz album or a scene out of *Akira*. He stared ahead at the faded lines on the road that disappeared into near-Milanese darkness. He was processing all his thoughts into English bite-size pieces. I could tell by his expression. Only the inner conjugation of verbs does that to people's faces. He looked like a few guys I had always wanted to fall in love with- or people I had fallen in love with who hadn't returned the sentiments. Right then and there I was filling in his life story details and mysteries with all my silly romantic ideas. I couldn't shake the impression that he was like some prince out of a Shakespeare play or some haughty duke. It was only broken when he smiled and I could see his heart pretty plainly in his lips.

"Solange is quite a person- very unique."

"Yeah, she's really been great to me. We lost a mutual

friend recently and that's how we met."

"That would be Mr. Kevin. He was a sweetheart. Never showed up on time though- ever."

"Yeah. You knew him? He was my best friend." I felt about sixteen here. And stupidly ignorant about my supposed 'best' friend.

"Well I never slept with him- I'm healthy like an ox if that is buzzing around in your head." It was, actually, but ouch.

"I met him a few times. Very sweet guy. I am sorry for your loss."

"I didn't know you had met him. Solange didn't say anything about that."

"She's living so fast and in so many places at once, I cannot imagine she can remember everything that happens to her. She's one of the only old-style jetsetters I know. I don't know how she does it. But she is always in the right place at the right time."

"In the right clothes too."

"She's very conscious of the surfaces of life. Sometimes I think she is like those people in the desert that can see where the water is under the sand simply by looking at what is on the surface. She finds hidden things. A good talent to have, to be sure. If she has a hunch I tend to take notice. She gives good advice. Business-wise at least."

"I know just a little more about her than I know about you." I laughed saying that but I also felt a little weird too. Anxious even. Where the hell was I? And why? Or yeah, then his face reminded me.

"She doesn't like to talk about herself. I don't think she has a desire to. She knows how to keep quiet and listen. Good trait. But she's had an interesting go of it so far. She's been married a few times. Rich Italian bankers. The settlements, I am sure, were quite fat and generous. She's still on speaking terms with them. I met her through one of them actually. Got her a modeling job after the horror movies dried up."

"Ah, dirt- finally. How many husbands are we talking about here?"

"Two that I know of. Big fat moneymaking guys. She needs someone beautiful and young now. Someone that matches her body and brain."

"I agree."

"And that certainly won't be you! I need someone young and beautiful now myself too." He smiled and looked over at me with a quick nervous 47 year old jerk of the head. He put his hand on my knee to steady his joke. He didn't look his age. He was cheesy but I forgave him.

"You don't look your age."

"Ah! That bitch." He sounded in mocked mock pain. "She told you my age. It sucks to be getting this old when I feel like I wasn't even getting a chance to be young."

"Sorry, but you don't look old at all."

My brain was emptying like an unplugged bathtub. Too much information, so I was purging, I guess.

"What will you do with Solange? Her show sounds too –

what's the word- derivative. That can't be her."

"Oh I think that depends on the subject matter. She wants to interview you, talk about your restaurant and stuff."

"But I am so boring. I don't live any glamorous lifestyle anymore. I meet models. I manage their careers. Sometimes I sleep with them." He looked quickly at me and laughed. "But mostly I just sign checks. I don't run my life."

"Sounds interesting to me." At least more so than working an office job in Boston.

"Well I guess we all have our ideas of interesting. I want to go away for a while. The restaurant can be so stressful; it isn't a quiet out of the way place. It has a reputation and it needs a lot of attention from everyone to make sure it stays up on all the best and shit."

He slowed down at the toll booth. A metal box slung on his front passenger seat visor beeped as we passed the booth.

"That's cool."

"Yeah it makes the commute much faster than having to stop. So John, allora, what now? What are you doing in this country?" It was a big question and he put it out as a joke that he had the punch line to. I had no idea what to say.

"I want to have a good time doing something that I enjoy." That was such an American answer. In hindsight it was the right one.

"And a good time is defined by? Food, sex? A person to be with? Si, I have a hard time with this questions myself." His eyes darted around. "It isn't fair that you can look at me all you want and I have to keep my eyes on the road."

"Yeah right."

"Whaaat? You are a cute guy. Much younger looking than Solange described."

"Oh I didn't know Solange was talking me up. What did she say?"

"You have a weird sense of yourself John-boy."

"And you have non-weird sense of me? Or was that Solange's words?"

"All day I deal with guys that primp and preen and you get really numb to good looking people. Sometimes it takes someone who is new and different to make things click."

"I'm no model." I can live with positives and negatives of that declaration just fine. I think.

"Exactly. And it is nice to know that you don't want to be one."

"How do you know that?"

"You don't, do you?"

"No, God no- not that I could anyway. Kevin and I went to this New Year's Party for the Ford Agency when we were 19 years old. Everyone there gave us the once-over. I felt like a piece of meat. Our friend Candy said it was because we were new. The new boys. But we weren't- we were just going to the party."

There had been an inflatable dinosaur with a Santa hat on at that party. People were taking Polaroids with it until Kevin popped it with his cigarette by accident. We left hurriedly after that- nicking a bottle of champagne in the process.

"It's a strange business. It can be fun and exciting, mostly it can be demoralizing. The way it messes with people's heads can be unattractive. Especially an attractive head. But it is nice to know that you are not coming home with me to be a model."

Nope, I'm coming home with you to take off clothes, not to sell them.

"I don't use people to get ahead. That's probably why I was still in Boston where Solange found me."

"So its up to Solange huh? Sorry, so it's Solange's fault?"

"No, it's just that I wasn't doing anything."

"And you decided to take up Solange on her offer to let you use her to get ahead." Chuckle now, Milanese prince, I have plans for you.

"I guess you could see it that way. I didn't. I figured I could do something new and get away for a while."

"Then I guess I am part of the new. We'll see huh?"

The car was American- I am so bad with car makes.

"Why did you buy an American car?"

"Why would I sleep with an American guy?"

Blunt, much.

We passed pale thin trees growing in long uniform rows.

"Those get replanted every few years when they cut them down for paper. It's a cool thing- the look of it, no?"

Giacomo drove faster than anyone I have ever ridden in a car with. It was rocket-like, a no-moments-lost-in-this-commute kind of thing.

The car lights spread among the trees. The silence and the speed and the closeness of Giacomo supercharged me. The trees whipped in the wind by the car. The wind at the windows of the car. I could see his sharp determined face, hands rock at the wheel. He drove me away from everything that was meaningless in my life and further into his heart. There are no streetlights. Just that quiet night.

I wanted him to just keep driving. Keep going and maybe that could be our life. Just an endless drive. "Night Flights" by David Bowie. That kind of ambient synth wash in the background. Kings of an empty 4 am world. Bullshit like that.

And then finally the sound of the car slowing suddenly, the engine shifting and existence coming back so loud that it was silence, a white silence that ate the world. Industrial city lights were now losing their as-seen-from-the-Hubble-Telescope distant quality. They were coming on strong with semi-precious crystalline colors. Urban backbone shapes in the shadows. The outskirts of Milan whirred suddenly into view, tossing out its confusing streets at the car, octopus-like- trying to grasp a shell. Turning down that exit all my ESP was shut off. I couldn't see ahead anymore. I had no idea what I was getting myself into. It made me scared, excited too. My prescience was gone. I was a gay Paul Atreides unable to get his spice to flow.

The city was still day-warm, heavy with summer sighs and lit from within like a fire behind cracked amber glass. It had that vibe that made me feel like we were the only people alive. The rest of the people were gone. Banished. Desolate.

Romantic.

His apartment was empty. It was well furnished, but empty. It was actually three old apartments that he bought and blew out the walls. So the windows on the far wall inside faced both the inside of the courtyard and the back alley. Attached to these windows were small terraces, barely enough for some potted plants which his mother watered when she was down from the country.

"What a beautiful place that I will never live in."

"Che cosa?"

"Nothing Giacomo, just being flip."

"Ok, flipping guy."

I guess I have a knack for setting myself up for letdown. Later I learned that before he met me he did not want me to see his apartment. He had not wanted to meet me. Or it could have been Ruggero being jealous and telling Solange that shit.

His kitchen was huge; it could have been a restaurant kitchen. It was all too big for a single man. It was a kitchen that said really loud "I have money to spend on stuff I will never use." The kitchen table had a pile of mail on it addressed to an Italian woman's name. I figured it was his mom.

Three bedrooms, two baths. A Spartan living room sprawled out with floor-to-ceiling doors that led out to small terraces. A lot of plants. The whole place felt like a cat waiting for something to happen. It just hadn't yet.

Giacomo took my jacket. He made a short tour of the place.

"Here is my mother's room when she visits from Romagnese which is north of here." It was a nun's room. Clean, simple, if a little cold. More of the mail was in this room so I guessed right I supposed. "Here's my room- which doubles as the guestroom." He laughed at his little joke before I realized what he was talking about.

He carried himself like he had known me for a hundred years.

A huge built-out wardrobe had been installed against the long wall facing his bed. A big closet that could fit a half dozen people. Its size and placement gave the impression that it was going to swallow the bed, maybe even the whole room.

He flicked on his stereo, the kind of tiny one piece stereo that people who don't listen to a lot of music have.

"Something's Pulling Me Under' filled the room. Nice soundtrack for our fucking, which blurred into a hot mash of mouth, arms, legs and the stuff between. Clumsily we pulled away all the clothes. There was some sand or dirt on the wood floor- it pressed against my back, cold and random. His tongue was the same temperature as my mouth. Always a good sign

Uncut cock aimed at my mouth like some half-melted heat-seeking torpedo. I figured that most Italians drop a lot of top talk but they end up being bossy bottoms. I figured mostly right.

I looked at the bag of rubbers in his nightstand. They were all about three years old. I needed to make a quick trip.

Fucking can be many things to many people. For me- it's almost like sign language or Braille or something. People talk through their bodies and their sex and it's a private kind of language that no one can be taught- it's what they've seen in movies, read in books and seen in art mixed with all their dreams of prince charming and endless heaven fueled cum-spouting juggernauts of being.

My hands were under his back and on his ass cheeks- getting sweaty and tired from pulling closer- unable to make certain atoms merge and attain perfect concentric orbits, perfect rhythms. His face was liquid, first in pain, then joy. Like someone who thought they were shot but realized they had not been. Just a cock pushing past all the defense and stress held in a sweaty butt. Battery acid burned out in a salt wash dead sea of Mexican spice vapors. Or Indian, curry armpit aroma, moans.

I supported his ass in my left hand between his ball sac and butt hole. His cock blurred in the frenzy of his right hand whacking. I slipped a finger into him as he got close. Sweaty, like an Italian gym teacher- still got his sneakers on.

Afterwards, he did the same for me. I had never really been fucked until him. I was magically transformed I guess. I could take it for what it was. All of it too.

My head can't get around that now but at the time it was so hot. Moving along the rhythm that only we had of the pressure of his hard-on and my dick pushing out the long lines of sensation all through our bodies in some weird nude massage class.

We had that kind of sex where your inner Midi synth starts doing the porno music but then abruptly slows down to a soul grumbler, to a sound that is almost a voice that almost says, in an almost familiar voice: "You've found another piece of yourself in someone else." And all you can do is smile, in the dark, in his arms.

I had a dream that I'd been walking in a diorama of what life was like in the early 21st century. That suddenly a volcano or a flash ice age had wiped out the city I am in- but remarkably preserves my body and the clothes and numerous mundane accessories, all the bookmarks of this pathetic culture, so that some future hole-digger might find out that I was in love and shining in the year of our lord etc ad nauseum. My life is spread out in a museum. It's sudden importance due to the fact that it was found intact. A minute spore of the whole of culture expanded to the universal voice. All my flaws would be magnified into earth-shattering theory breakers concerning dental health, gender determined fashion, globalization (the future finders sneer) and pollution. My life acquired a silent solemnity, like now, next to Giacomo, perhaps that was the stillness that brings on these thoughts. The distance between us held the sounds of museum doors closed, exhibit ticket stubs swept away and the lights- they had been flicked off.

Silence. The sheets had slid a bit, had made a slow shiver run through him. The sun-faded fabric that covered the open bedroom window moved softly in a gentle morning breeze. The light came through it, picking up a pink-orange cast. Somewhere in the apartment, the phone rang three times. It echoed in the flat metallically. The answering machine clicked and an artificial voice, like an old Speak 'n Spell programmed in Italian, proclaimed the lack of Giacomo and his willingness to return your call. Beep.

A familiar woman's voice rolled out in weirdly accented Italian. After a few long sounding sentences, she switched to English. It was Solange. I bolted upright. Giacomo stirred but didn't wake up.

"Ciao John, I'm off to Roma for a few days for some business stuff- no worries- chill with Ruggero and Giacomo and I will collect you later when I get back. I know you must be thinking there she goes again but this is like my lifestyle so best to break you in quick and dirty! I left some euros for you in Pavia. You are right, that *Angel* song by Gavin Friday is great. I knew I'd heard it before- it was on the Romeo and Juliet

- 118 -

soundtrack. Make sure to pick up a cell phone too. Ask Giacomo about that. I may have some cool news about a film festival in Cairo when I get back. Baci, ciao bello, later!"

Before I could get out of bed or even think to find out where the sound was coming from, she had hung up. She had given me the slip again. I was beginning to wonder what I was going to put on my tax returns as employment, if anything.

I headed back to bed. Giacomo was face down, pillows prompted around his ears to kill the sound. The sheets had pulled up along his legs. His ass had no hair on it. One leg was off the side of the bed against a little table's leg.

On the table was a framed picture. The decoy girl. She stood in the photograph with wide eyes, had watched us all night. She was a time traveler; that girl that he must have fucked a million years ago b.c. She's like the patron saint of my Italian sex life- St. Tiny Northern Italian Mountainous Village Girl. She'd spied us as we made a mess of his new bed. He was so proud to say that I was the only guy he has ever had sex with in it. Christened with a one-night stand. Of course I had to ask him how long he has had said bed.

Three weeks. What a record.

But back to the girl- that would probably be the farthest thing from her dreams- her little Giacomo banging (and banged by) some Americano (no need to add 'boy' there cuz it's a masculine noun- got that down going down) in the year of our lord.

Anyway, he was still asleep, still naked and still snoring.

But I didn't mind for some reason. His eyes were closed, obviously, as sleep does that- but there was this thing in his face while he slept. As if he was in pain or being fucked or just confused. Probably just confused, poor baby. I used to think that if you stared at someone while they slept you would see their true face. I don't believe that anymore. I think if you keep you eyes open while everyone is awake you can pretty much figure out what someone's true face is. It's all about being awake- not about sleeping at all.

I watched him go through the motions of some abduction. He was standing in my the middle of my heart now, like a sexy crossing guard unsure of the flow of traffic but giving it his best try. Where do we go, sir?

I was a bit pissed at Solange, but I was also happy to stay with Giacomo. But I needed some cash.

I got up, dressed, watched Giacomo get ready for work.

"I'm going to go back to Pavia to get that money Solange left me."

"Va bene, I can come get you tonight or you can come back on the bus. There is a little breakfast for you in the fridge, you can have whatever you want in there. Wait." He gave me a kiss and grabbed a pen from the blue enamel kitchen table. He jotted down some stuff on a piece of paper. "These are the directions to the bus and the stop to ask for it you get lost. Okay, now I go."

He grabbed a bag from the chair that had "Eyes Model Management" stenciled on it.

"That get you laid a lot?"

"When I am desperate, yes."

He smiled and I almost believed him.

Door click, now food.

I found a good half-eaten panini-type leftover and some sparkling water in his refrigerator. I tossed that in my bag. I crossed the courtyard and then slid into the street.

I sat in the park behind Sempione with the hot air wafting up through my shorts- all the air was humming with a soft mortal summer light as it spun slowly up into noon. It was a lazy day and I gradually made my way to the bus station.

The bus chugged along the tiny stream that strung Milano to Pavia for a good ten miles. The sky's reflection went skittering across it. The morning's painkiller had vaporized my personality. It ricocheted throughout my whole brain. I'd stupidly left the directions that half-conscious Giacomo had scribbled on a shred of newspaper at the apartment.

The sun was hard on my skin as I got off the bus. I smelled of warm skin and condoms. Almost sexy this early in the morning and the blood had started to remember what it was supposed to do in time to stop my brain from shutting down altogether.

Well there I was and the street clotted full of people. For such a small town there shouldn't have been anyone there but it teemed. Teeming, this Pavia and all around is a kind of cinnamon cloud of old worldness. It's sexy in a dry powder form. Just add sweat.

The door lock buzzed like trapped wasps in a hot metal box and opened. The decadent foliage of Ruggero's apartment hung around me coolly. His maid made me coffee. Marco was at work and Ruggero was sitting with a cigarette by his computer, typing in staccato bursts.

"Ciao John. Was the sex very good?" His round face mooned me briefly- then revolved back to the screen.

"Umm yeah. Thanks."

"Giacomo is charming. He is a charmer when he wants to be. Solange left you some money in an envelope in the guest bedroom. You can stay here of course, I love the company. Or in Milano as I am sure you will anyway."

He said nothing about the way I looked which was good because I looked like a 15 year old without a good meal, dark circles under the eyes. Save the Children.

I visualized a vague kind of life here in Italy for me. It was like a crossword spread out before me. I just had to fill in all the letters.

I spent the day wandering around Pavia with Ruggero looking at shops and buying clothes I probably couldn't get away with wearing outside of Italy. In the evening Giacomo got out of work and came to pick me up.

I felt more fuck-high and 'in touch with my Italian heritage' than ever before and with an all-too-familiar, childish pang, I realized I was probably in love. And so I passed two weeks, without Solange, an occasional reassuring phone call now and then to remind me that everything was okay. I took the time to learn the Milano subway system like a lattice of veins for my own love life support.

It amazes me that we go through our lives unable to see what we are doing. Like, everyone else can watch us moving around and stuff but we have no idea what kind of image we are presenting to the world. And I don't mean that in an ego-maniac way. I swear, if I hear another person complain about someone's honest self-introspection as being self-centered or egomaniac like in any way- I just hate that. How are we supposed to get on with our lives if we don't even have a clue what the fuck we are? And I love how they all go – hey grow up. Like getting old is going to make you suddenly an expert on something. And all the experts I have ever met are fucking assholes anyway. That's the thing about Solange. She reeks of somebody who knows a lot of stuff but she isn't running around telling me what to do or think or anything.

Sometimes people confuse confidence with being self-centered too. Especially with women. It is a sexist thing.

This from an Italian who fucks boys.

Anyway, the day was whittling down to a scant bit of penny colored splotches on the sky. I didn't want to think about anything. I was beginning to feel like I was being sucked back home like through some wind tunnel or something.

Fuck.

I should get drunk.

Hard to ignore the sounds of young Italians banging into things and each other outside tonight. It's a lonely sound. Not being amongst them and not being able to understand them even if I was.

I should get some wine. I wouldn't mind some serious slow time. I don't think that is in the cards.

Suffer suffer suffer. Waiting for Giacomo to buy rubbers. Slowly unrolling into the jacuzzi tub like a dirty snake. All the colors on the water at Como get dizzy acid trippy in the sunlight, like mother nature has some sad serious jones for Peter Max.

We got a table in the enclosed courtyard at his restaurant on Via Brisa. He was a partner in one of the newer, trendier restaurants, but this one was smaller. It was well known by locals as a beyond tasty well-kept secret. The wait staff got all-uptight and super professional when he walked in.

All smiles inside me as he described the way some obscure word was tainted by the English somewhere in the swamp of time.

"Language is a funny thing. If you can't speak the native language it is so easy to miss large pieces of that country's culture. Of course then there is an opportunity to teach you the words and the customs."

"That's an American's one best weapon with Europeans-listen and play the ignorant student. I do it.

"Italians especially love it. We like to talk about ourselves, our country, our history."

"I suppose it can be a huge turn off and also an aphrodisiac, depending on the person. I know that I can pull that out of my hat. It's a silly power I guess."

"Never really mastering a language gives everyday

conversations a strange edge."

"Commonplace can become sexy, sexy commonplace."

"Trust rarely takes place in language."

"Eyes? Smiles?"

"Yes, but beautiful smiles and beautiful eyes can trick you every time." His eyes were sheened with a warm light coming off the chandeliers. "Those are Murano glass, of Venice."

"Beautiful. So no place for trust?"

"It isn't easy. Not in my life."

Every so often the restaurant halted its conversations. Silence shuttered down along the tiny street running from the main road to that restaurant. It was dark because there were no streetlights but inside it seemed to be like Christmas if Christmas happened in late August.

"I'm about 6 hours into the future from all the people I left behind in Boston. Literally left them in the past."

"You are moving under your own power. A good feeling."

"Not really. I am moving under remote pilot from Solange."

"Yes, she can be a mystery. She is like the super woman. Always ahead of everyone." Giacomo smiled at the trays of food that settled in front of us. The wait staff was starched taut with anticipation. "But you shouldn't feel like you are doing nothing. Knowing Solange, perhaps you are working right now? No?"

My eyes rested on Giacomo. So soft and slow. What was next? Allora? Even the sky hunched down to get a good look at us. Trying to suss out our plots. The red wine was making my senses all stained glassed and rubber gloved. Red wine would really get the plot going. No doubt.

"Well it's a good job regardless of whether or not I know I am employed." I needed to have a word with that Solange.

After a dessert that reintroduced the meaning of the word 'chocolate' to my mouth, his face slowly warped with drunk tears. I hadn't realized how much wine we had drunk. It was like we had noticed all the same wounds in each other and had decided to anesthetize for some sort of soul surgery. I didn't want it, but there was not escaping it.

"I want to say more but I have no Italian vocabulary."

"If you just talk I am sure to understand you.

"I didn't want to get all serious and melancholy."

"It is the wine that makes us a little melancholy, that's all. Not our feelings for each other."

"Yeah." It was what I wanted to hear and what I feared because now I am stuck. Stuck in a place that only gets light from his eyes.

But the lights from his car pushed out across the ruins by the restaurant. No one in their wildest ravings back then could imagine the scenes that played out in front of these old pillars. Two boys, one an old boy at that, fighting something in them because they were drunk and in love but cannot see it all from the height they are at. And getting higher. Higher and higher, and then falling. I knew I was sure to fall somehow.

The car was parked in the lot. The dinner had not been digested.

"I can say all my hopes and dreams to you in Italian because you cannot understand them. Just the sound they make and even though you cannot understand what I say- it feels so good to be able to say them aloud in front of someone. Capito?"

"Capito."

We were so full from the restaurant food that we had decided to take a long walk. Streets of Milano by his apartment.

The street vendors had cheap rings for sale and his hands were on my shoulders. We were still moving but not forward or backward, like a paused CD. Anticipation and fearlessness. Outside in the night. Like a couple that has done this over and over again. But it's the first time. The bed was calling and calling.

The night was still pressing us together. We were walking down that street poking each other's erections and jumping back and away, laughing. The stars were out with cold blue light that almost hurt my head. The streets have that older than anything in New York feeling. Italy had blow darted my whole soul. I was numb with love, feeling no pain. Never a good sign, but that's my brain being a D.J., doing the remix for my heart.

I fucked Giacomo on the floor of his living room. The stereo was playing Dubtribe Soundsystem. We were being advised to "Do It Now." Hot breath on hot breath over skin.

Now, down into him. Clean, with no cologne. All natural smells. The best smelling guy on earth or at least that I've been with- take your pick. I wonder how much I will pay for this all in future hysterical H.I.V. paranoia but fast-forward...

I can see his age when he sits on me. I think he's lying about it too but that makes no sense- it doesn't matter. To make sense of the world by simply fucking it. Or simply just fucking it for the fuck of it.

He was ecstatic, saying something in Italian, laughing so hard. I couldn't understand him. I'll never forget the sound of his voice or the look of his face. Sunset was coming through the slats of blinds, throwing shadow lines on us. I could see tears standing in his eyes, reluctant little unknown soldiers almost ready to sacrifice themselves for the greater good. Then in my thrust he came and they sat in his eyes. Not a drop ran down his cheeks.

The wet streets of Milano after a short rainfall. The scene

was all done up nice like a birthday present sent to the wrong address.

I didn't want to fall in love. But I don't have a voice in those kinds of decisions. The atoms have their dance. They continue to bring us together until we get it right. And right means perfection and perfection, if I can paraphrase the delightfully life-affirming Sylvia Plath, is death.

I've really tried to make a conscious effort to keep the love stuff to a minimum in my life. Maybe without it we're better. More streamline. Less prone to breaking down. Not because I don't want it around, but because I get so tangled up in it. When I was younger I was falling in love all the time and it got to be a big pain- especially if the guy fell in love with me. Then it was all over. I mean- what is more pathetic than grown adults worrying about where the other is all day? Or is that co-dependent or something. Whatever, I mean I can't believe that that is abnormal – I think everyone is worried about their loved one. Where are they? Are they ok? Are they cheating on me? Do they care? My way is soo much easier. If it was any easier I swear I could be a hooker- I really could and then it would be making some money too. Ok yeah I am kidding on the hooker part. Small attachments here and there, but nothing overwhelming. Ya know, nothing that boils the brain chemistry too much. All these in-love people, like so much reduced butter. Boiling away. Or worse, getting burned.

The one thing I definitely want to steer clear of is obsession because I know that I am simply removing myself from my own life through an extreme focus on another. So obsessive love isn't really about love- it's a form of suicide. Although it can feel like love- I am sure it isn't.

The other thing is the way love can give you that feeling that you dreamt the whole thing? Ya know, you go through all the phone conversations and emails and letters all over again a million times to feel that glow and to remember that it all really happened and it is happening but yet you cant shake the feeling that it all was a dream – a really good R-rated dream- hopefully an arty hardcore film if you're really lucky. And then he calls and gives you a wake up jolt of reality. That can be sooo disorientating. And for me, well I need someone shouting my name at me all day so I can remember it let alone someone that wants a piece of ass as well.

Unless of course you just want to be a big slut. Then you've gotten a whole bunch of other things to consider. Starting with rubbers in bulk.

Solange came back to Milano that night, exactly two weeks to the day after leaving that messy message on Giacomo's Speak 'n Spell-voiced answering machine. Giacomo wanted to celebrate at his newer trendier restaurant. I got drunk early and it was a blurry vague warm kind of evening. Solange was show stopping, of course, in a wrap-around cotton jersey concoction, a la *Mahogany*.

Midway through the meal she disappeared with a busboy for a while. He was a hot Algerian guy with sexy cruel eyes cut with a warm coffee con leche smile. They were gone for about a half an hour and Giacomo kept laughing to himself.

"The service sucks here." Solange came back, adjusted her von Furstenberg.

"How well?"

"Don't you know, you hire them don't you Giacomo?"

"No, no, I am just a money bags. I don't do day to day!"

"That must explain your mood." Solange pouted and did her "primp face" to me as an aside.

There was a man sitting in the corner of the restaurant. He had a really bad fake tan, like the stuff they had before all the breakthroughs with the bronzers. Or maybe it was a skin condition. He was eyeing us up and down. He was like a preying mantis with a weight problem. He seemed to be giving Solange a thorough look over. I just figured that he was being a perv.

"That guy has been staring at you for about 20 minutes."

"No biggie. I might know him from somewhere or vice versa."

"He's kinda scary looking. Alain said some guy came around his place before we left looking for us. Description fits."

"Naw, I am sure he's fine, hang on."

She got up, took a smoke out and went over to him. He looked a bit startled and his eyes got wide and then quickly narrowed so you couldn't see the whites. He seemed to be saying something to Solange as she leaned in to light her smoke. When he stopped talking Solange looked at him right in the face with a blank expression, touched her earrings with her left hand and walked away without thanking him. She came up and put her arm around me with her back to his table.

"No, I don't know him. And I will make it a point to never."

I went to Pavia with Ruggero that night because Giacomo's mother was going to the doctor's in the morning and she was staying in Milano. In the morning a photo of Giacomo's restaurant was on the front page of the newspaper. Ruggero translated the article for me.

"It's a bit scandalous, also in the way it's written." He said, pawing at the paper from behind me. "It says that two people were made sick with, I don't know how to say in English- it's the food that made them sick. Very sick. But they are writing the article with a lot of insults. Not very objective."

"Are they alive?"

"One old lady died. The rest are at the hospital. They are alive but sick from the food." Ruggero made weird gestures around his eyes. "The poison is like the stuff in injections for women. For lines in the face."

"Botulism?"

"Si, the botox. They were poisoned by the food. Giacomo is going to be so upset by this."

"I can imagine."

The sun came in from the terrace filtered through the

green and ivory leaves woven into the drapes. I had no idea how Giacomo would take this news. He had not called Ruggero. I called Solange.

"Yeah I heard. It's crazy. I can't believe it. Good thing we didn't order any of whatever they had."

"Is it going to be really bad?"

"It depends. The place is spotless. The kitchen is state of the art. I can't imagine how that could have happened. It's rare. We'll have to see. It could have been from a supplier. Who knows. Kinda puts that segment of the show out of commission, huh?"

"What are you doing?"

"I'm in Milano, I got a hotel room and I am shopping now."

"I'm coming back to Milan. I want to see if Giacomo is ok. You don't think that is a bad idea do you?"

"No I am sure he would enjoy your concern. He loves that kind of attention. Maybe you can find out what happened. It's such a scandal."

I took the next little bus to Milan with a bag of snacks that Ruggero packed for me.

From the bus station I walked down the long, ancient Milanese sidewalks, slicked gray- pocked with shiny dark circles and oblongs, like month-old fucked-on sheets. Just getting outside in a busy city was good. I've never been this blanked before. Like a bird that they keep a little hood on to calm it or to make it manageable. Maybe I am being made manageable. Maid Manageable.

Giacomo's powerful Italian spells clung to me. My brain had withered in his Novocain or whatever he used to cut his personality. He doesn't know much about me really. Just my shoe size and the smile I suppose. Oh yes and he 'thinks I may be a poet." I guess it would take someone named Giacomo to say that about me. Go back on 'pause.'

This walk served no real purpose. I was just rewinding all the stuff I've done with him- but without him, he's spliced out and set apart. Don't flunk the astrology portion of the romantic obsession test. It's much harder than the oral and it's truly subjective. Know your test giver.

My sloppy heart- as the song goes- is now just a bundle of blue. Whenever I feel its beat I get kinda crazy. He's always saying he can feel my pulse all through my body. I wonder why I can't trust him. It's difficult to separate instinct from paranoia- but I think maybe that is what makes us human in some weird way. So on that aspect maybe I have sunk to subhuman. Although I am probably more delusional than paranoid. I think I was having some sort of delayed stress reaction from the Paris restaurant. My legs cut out from under me a few times and I got a scrape on my face. Or maybe my fate was mixing with my new acquaintances.

Back on the street and dodging a car cuz I've been too walled up in my head on this walk – an old ziti-skinned man yells at me in Italian – from the circumstance (and my total lack of Italian language skills) he must be angry that I nearly walked into his moving car- so I just bow my head and meekly try to evacuate the scene. He's not convinced that I have been humiliated enough so he pressed his face closer to me and breathed on me. I warded him off with shrugged shoulders.

Beetle-red, shiny Discman was a saving grace. The words and the breath bounce off Dubtribe Sound System-- "Be fearless, do it now"-- and fail to connect with any important memories of the day. Everything is between my legs today.

Well maybe not everything. I was a little hungry and that could be cause for panic because I was alone, had already gone through all the Ruggero snacks and the language thing really was starting to get to me. It is different than being in language class in high school because I had absolutely no desire to learn German. But Italian? It's a powerful magic on the ears and heart. I'd like to acquire its soft seductive words. Even clichés can make you cum. A good thing to remember on lonely nights.

Lonely nights reminded me of Alain and then I felt terrible that he was probably sitting somewhere eating delivery pizza because he was too scared to go to a restaurant. Or be in public. And that reminded me of the whole shooting thing. My brain had been trying to degauss that, but it kept surfacing like a body on a beach.

I know my wandering has a purpose because there was Porta Ticinese, straddling ahead of me. It isn't an imposing piece of gate at all. It was raised to celebrate some victory of Napoleon's and ended up being re-dedicated to peace. Not that it had worked. It's like a broken stuffed animal now.

I liked the smell here too, open and weathered. The gelateria here is really good so I get some. The staff gives me a weird look so I must look a little sweaty and dazed.

The Italian sky was falling down now; fading in a slow, cracked amber-glass haze. It was a dusky, dusty place. The Milanese streets made no sense and seemed to rename themselves whenever I turned around. It's hypnotic though. The cinnamon cigarette stained pull of it was everywhere, as if the city knows my name or makes the sounds of some warm safe pre-birth time. Dizzy in the head from familiarity, from this black hole in my head. Cindy's crushed skull sledding.

I wanted to be a little lost. A little out of the way. Just slightly away from the place I should be. I got really lost and ended up walking for about an hour and a half.

I asked directions from an elderly lady. She stared at me with a long wide scared face and pointed to the streets and made gestures. I kept saying, "prego" instead of 'grazie." The old lady just stared at me like I was dog shit. I'd forgotten I was looking a bit shell-shocked.

I found the flat again, exactly where I left it. Bits of the neighborhood were sticking in my memory now. Soon the whole place will open out like a flower gone past full bloom.

I was late for dinner. Giacomo was a bit upset until he really looked at me. I looked like I had been sweating in a field all day. A lot of Italian came flying out of his mouth and he grabbed to hug me. Ouch. I told him about the restaurant and the suicide performance art. I left out the part about Alain and all our fucking. The nights on his terrace in the rain and wearing nothing but condoms around his flat.

Giacomo ran a bath in the big fancy jet tub he had and bathed me. I was trembling. I felt like I had been dunked in a warm cup of Alka Seltzer. I think I fainted or fell asleep or went into shock. I kept mumbling that the cigarette was going to burn down the restaurant. But I didn't dare get up. I'd get shot.

Solange called while I was sleeping. Giacomo was acting like a nurse, getting me water and holding my hand. Giacomo Romeo Rodolpho is quite a bunch of names, aye? He told her that I would call her later. That I was asleep.

"Eyes without A Face" on the radio now. I was drifting in the sunlight that streamed in from the back windows of his flat. After we had post traumatic syndrome sex (which consisted of him holding me down- which I kinda like- and giving me a tongue implant) I got out of bed. I washed my hands and toweled the sweat off me. I looked in the medicine cabinet for some aspirin and did mirror faces until he yelled at me to come back to bed. I have no idea what binds us together and I hope somehow we avoid discovering it too soon. I don't want to lose him to that everyday feeling. But it hunted me. It will get at me eventually.

The day was hot and thick with summer. All the smells in the street were coming through the windows. Even though Giacomo had the place rewired he haven't gotten around to buying an air conditioner. I don't like them anyway. And I hate when I am in New York and they sputter and spit me on as I walk down the street.

When I woke up the next day I called Solange back. I told her about the shooting in the French restaurant finally.

"What?" She was scared that I was having some sort of residual karmic effect.

"I went to a restaurant." I almost giggled that out, like a nervous psychologically damaged kid. Or not like at all. "While you were away, I went to eat with some new people in Paris and then they started shooting themselves. Made a big mess."

"Are you shitting me?"

"No."

"And it was in an American-style restaurant? What the hell were you doing trying to eat American food in Paris?"

"I deserved it huh?" I laughed a little, tried to be "light."

"I think I heard about that in the news. And you didn't tell me because?"

"I didn't want to get you upset or feeling weird."

She got strangely quiet.

"How about I take you to Berlin? I want to get some ideas for more shows and really start working. It's hard to get anything done in Italy- with all the fucking and eating going on."

"Berlin sounds cool."

Giacomo looked up at me curiously, an almost hurt look on his face.

Solange's phone call was full of white noise. White noise from a black girl. I felt like a guy who hadn't called a woman he'd promised to keep in touch with. The walls in Giacomo's flat must have been made out of some crazy material. My cell phone usually didn't sound like this. Although, Solange could have been in Cambodia for all I knew.

"I'll be back in Milan tomorrow- I'm sorry I'm such a terrible boss." She sounded concerned and also relieved. Her voice had no Mouseketeer in it, like Kevin would say. Maybe she thought I was mad at her or blamed her.

"I'm not alone Solange."

"Yes you are. I will be there in the morning. I bought the tickets for Berlin already anyway. We can start writing some of the story ideas and we can decide what places to profile."

She was like an ad for normal. She was going to make sure that I was ok.

Giacomo was ready to go off to work at the office when Solange was expected to arrive. He came into the kitchen clutching his little model manager bag and a folder of photographs.

"Look at this new guy we could sign for the agency."

I looked at the contact sheets. He looked vaguely familiar. He seemed a little too 'model-y' for my tastes.

"Doesn't he look like you? " Giacomo whipped the sheets out of my hand. "Especially here and here."

"I don't look like him at all."

"Yes you do, only he is younger and cuter."

"Thanks."

"Kidding bellooooo." He drew that last syllable in 'bello' out into a long sigh.

"Don't you guys do digital photography over here yet?"

"Not for this stuff, no."

Buzz. The intercom door thing was migraining for attention.

"Si, who's that girl?" Giacomo sang into the mesh.

"Giacomo it's your dark star." Did she even know what

dark star meant? I think not.

Buzz. Solange whipped up the stairs. I noted she was familiar with the place.

We ciao'd Giacomo and went to a café and had espresso outside. The wind was warm. She had on black Gibbon sandals and a new Roberto Cavalli skirt and mesh top thing that looked great on her.

She broke down when she took a long moment to look at me. Real tears and everything. As long as I had known her I had felt that she was always moments away from confessing some amazing double life. She was too fantastic to not be an Israeli operative or some international drug czarina. Just like Kevin I had begun to fantasize about her life, making up stories about what she did when I wasn't around. It wasn't like she was distant or aloof and it wasn't that she seemed to be anymore deceptive than most of the people I knew. I just couldn't decide if she was holding back parts of her life to conceal them from me or to make me feel like there was some sort of mystery surrounding her. That she was more interesting than she actually was, if that makes any sense. Whichever it was, it worked. It was magnetic. The desire to know all her secrets was addictive. Maybe that is the mark of a truly great actor.

Sobbing, she confirmed all of my craziest, wildest mental tangents. I think she had some weird idea that the shooting had something to do with her. She seemed to be crying out of guilt, not out of fear for my psychological well-being. Then in the midst of her shuddering, shivering crying jag:

"I poisoned the food at Giacomo's restaurant."

"What?"

I could hardly understand her words. It was like hearing second hand that you had won a lottery or been sentenced to the electric chair. I had waited so long for something exciting to happen and there it was- it was happening and I didn't have any idea as to whether I was ready for it- and that was part of the thrill.

Everything about Solange that I had thought was over the top suddenly came into focus. The heightened sense of melodrama made sense. And after a bit of thinking, it wasn't so surprising. I am sure that somehow I had caught a whiff of her off-kilter diligence. Then I realized that I was the tourist in her world- she was normal here. I was the alien. She was living in her natural environment and I had only been issued a visa. She was camouflaged perfectly. I was the one dressed wrong, heart pinned to sleeve.

"What do you mean you poisoned the restaurant?"

"Ssshhh!" She sshh'd me louder than we had been talking. "The chef at Giacomo's restaurant. I was hired to ruin him. I was paid to destroy him, his reputation. And then in about eight months he is going to be killed. I just had to slip some food poisoning, some botulinum toxin into the seafood that had been given me."

"What the fuck are you talking about?"

"I do jobs."

"Jobs?"

"Jobs that most people don't want to do. I get paid to fuck with people. Sometimes, well actually most times, people get hurt." She looked like some sort of water sprite- so many tears were coming down the sides of her cheeks. Water, water everywhere. Big shocker, Solange had killed people for money. She'd practiced making other people's beds. She'd shined shoes for morticians. She'd put people on crash diets. Solange was something of a diva of Death.

"Solange- what the fuck? That old lady died."

"Chefs here in Europe kill themselves over their reputation. Something like this is a career stopper." I guess the old lady was on the way out too. Regardless- Solange never mentioned her or replied to my line of questioning.

"No, not that. Why did you bring me here? What am I doing here?"

"That's the thing, sweetheart. I am so sorry." Shiver shudder, sniffle. "I don't know why you are here. I mean, I needed someone here and Kevin was gone and I couldn't do everything without someone being here."

"Kevin knew about this? About your work?"

"Yeah. He knew everything. When he got sick I knew that

I was going to be alone with all these secrets. I don't know how to explain it to you. He was like my absolver."

"He took your confessions? So I am like Kevin's stand-in? I need to drink."

"Good idea. We can get anything you want. I have a lot of money John. I get so much money from the things I do and it's never enough."

I wanted to grab her by the arms and tightly shake her. Feel her bones through her flesh in my hands and wake her up. What was she doing to my life? What had I done to get involved in all this? I was suddenly stuck in a noir thriller. Larger then life cast, glamorous locations. No soul. I was erased. The back of my legs felt weak.

"The chef at Giacomo's fucked with some girl. The girl's fiancé and her uncle hired me to destroy him. It's a very basic revenge job. Usually it's for money, like sometimes people don't pay so they get someone like me to mix it up a bit." She did a weird kind of nervous self-effacing kind of smirk. "The people who hire me want a certain amount of pain and fear to be doled out- with finesse."

"And for some reason you know how to do this?" I was trying to picture her at some school for wayward divas searching for murderess training. "How does someone get qualified for this line of work."

"I have an overactive imagination and I'm detailed oriented." If she had been a cynical, world weary anti-heroine that would have been funny. Now it just seemed scary and honest. "And when I was 16 I dated this Italian who taught me all this crazy stuff. It was a ticket away from a pretty gnarly life."

The way I'm sure Solange sees it is that these people are going to die anyway, she is hired to kill them so if she didn't do it some one else would, so she isn't actually killing them, her employer is. It's like working at McDonalds, you serve people hamburgers but you don't actually kill and cut up the cows. It's like if that guy would cut off his pregnant wife's head had hired Solange to do it. He would still be guilty of the murder. She enjoys it too, she feels like she has a purpose. Maybe she's Robin Hood.

"I'm sorry." She was sincere, too, although her tears had automatically dried and her makeup had recharged somehow, like a director had said cut and reset the scene.

"What do you mean you're sorry? I haven't done anything. I'm not in danger am I?" Suddenly I felt scared that I was guilty by association, by fascination. First degree voyeurism.

"No, not at all. I just feel so horrible about dragging you to Europe just to make you my little father confessor."

"Solange. I was bored. I wanted to come." Although I don't know what I would have done if I had known the truth.

"Yeah." She stared into space. Her eyes had a shiny glass-like quality about them- blank, like she had decided to conserve energy for her brain and was doing a lot of internal diagnostics. Her lips were the only emotional ambassadors from that interior landscape. She had become as serious as I had ever seen her. As serious as when she had to decide what to do next after the rats had attacked in *Rat Attack!* In that case, she quoted the Bible and ended up getting gnawed on. No such luck this time.

"I think you should get away from Giacomo. I don't know how much he knows but he is a dangerous man. He got his money in a hundred ways that you would never want to hear about. I did more than model for him back in the day. I just don't want him to get back at me through you."

"Well that's a little late sweetheart. If one of us were a girl we would be picking out names by now."

"Fuck." The way she said that word reminded me of licorice. I can't explain it, but when she said it I could taste it. "I don't know what to say about that. Maybe Giacomo just likes you. Who wouldn't?"

"I really like Giacomo."

"You'll get over it." As simple as putting new toilet paper in the bathroom. "He's a killer too."

She was pretty flippant, like a regular TV Guide of blasé.

"So everyone you know is a killer?"

"He isn't a killer like I - wait, I wanna rephrase that cuz I don't think of myself as a killer."

"Oh, okay."

I wish I could tell her that I really felt for him. I got a really guilty feeling about being unable to tell her that I felt closer to him now than her, that I knew all the weird manipulations she'd been pulling with me in a subconscious way-- not that Solange has any right to be questioning my motives.

"Thanks." I felt like my heart had been three-hole-punched and slung in a loose-leaf binder.

"Do you think he suspects anything? Is he really close with the chef?"

"I don't know. I'm really stupid. I should never have taken a job so close to people I know. It was the challenge. I feel like an idiot but really it's the challenge. It's a rush."

"Let's try to take into account my life when you are going for the gusto from now on, okay? At least while I am here in Europe and people are being introduced to me through you?"

"I'm sorry." She was still wiping tears away although they had stopped gushing a while back. She had shed her disguises tonight. It was like being let in on a magician's secret but not being disappointed. She was far more human and real than I had ever given her credit for. I can't say it wasn't exciting. Half of me wasn't even repulsed by this revelation. Or maybe I was still in shock. Although, I guess I wanted to be in this kind of insane homicidal drama. I needed to balance my internal violence with the external. Why else would I have offered to continue to help her?

"If you can so easily accept the bad you must make room for the occasional joy, no?"

Giacomo said it so smoothly, "occasional joy." We were dancing and getting drunk at this all-night party in a huge tent that had suddenly appeared off to the side of the road. At least that is how I remember it. Definitely not what Solange had meant when she said "Get away from Giacomo."

The Po River, flat as a planarian, gave off gray imitations of the moon. For the moment, nothing else existed- we were on a highway without any other traffic- empty and sun blinded- speeding through it all day. Waiting to crash or to take off into orbit.

And I should believe it- he might not be lying. And I do feel the magnetic pull of love, tugging at the iron in my blood. That was what truth was- the feeling that something means something to ones' self as opposed to something that comes from someone else's lips. Besides, if I were kissing him he couldn't talk anyway- so kiss, I guess would be my advice.

I was failing to remove my heart but I was also trying to figure out how to get information out of Giacomo. Did he know anything about what Solange had done? How could I ask without asking? And should I?

"I want you to be happy." He smiled putting his arms around me.

"The restaurant is a bad situation. Are you going to be okay?"

"I have to find out why the seafood that was used was bad and how that could have been sold to us. It's a big scandal. But you shouldn't be upset. You seem a bit upset. I want you to really enjoy. This will probably ruin the chef and the restaurant but it will not touch me. I will not let it touch me. And you should get happy. This place is very cool, no?"

Unfortunately my happiness was tied up in two people's vendettas and a former model turned contract killer and neither of them were in my employ. So it's a little difficult to be happy Giacomo. Just a little.

"It's been a weird time, this time in Italy. You've given me a really good time, Giacomo. And I'm not too much of a good luck charm." A flash of Pas De Chance from Cocteau's *Le Livre Blanc* bonked me in the head. "I just feel a little lost in space."

"You aren't lost. You're here with me. We have fun."

"Fun." I repeated it like an amen at the end of a prayer.

He bent down with his drink and put his lips close to my ear. "You fucked me, in the ass. I have only done this with one other man. This means something, no?"

"It means Giacomo, that you like to get fucked by someone who knows how to."

He giggled.

Ok, so maybe it means some other stuff too, but that stuff is better verbalized than sodomized, don't you think? Think, think, not the verb we mastered together. No, that would be to far down the alphabet for us, which you remind me, in Italian has no X or J. So no ex-boyfriends and no John's I suppose.

"Yeah it means a lot to me." I smiled, drank. I had to tell him that I was leaving. Not why I was leaving but that I was going, but I had no idea how to do that.

I'd been teetering on the edge of that decision. I couldn't help but feel like those people who play wine glasses. Yeah, exactly- completely irrelevant and obscure but somehow- musical. And that strange sound they make too. Yup that's me. A wet wine glass under someone's finger. But I'm remixing my metaphors.

"I have to go with Solange to work on the show."

He looked at me and nodded. Even his nod was in Italian.

"It's ironic that Solange brings both good luck and bad with her food travels. Because I would never have met you otherwise."

Our faces were so sore from kissing that our skin was dry and peeling. "I want to take you to the beach before you leave with Solange."

It had rained earlier, before we left the tent and got into his American car. It smudged the gray of the highway with silver just before dawn. And then the sun interrupted, dropping gold into the road.

We packed for the beach like it was any other day that I would be there. As if it happened every summer. John in Italy- oh yeah normal and not at all something that was slowly draining away. I wouldn't be looking back at this mournfully years from now drinking shitty merlot and crying to dumb songs we sang along to in the car- no not me. Ha ha ha. Whatever.

The road to Monterosso al Mare was twisted; full of little green stops and starts where grass and flowery plants rioted out along the cliff sides. Any one of the corners that we took at maximum velocity could have been the end- fiery wreckage hurtling down end over end to be wrapped in the sheets of a foamy blue Mediterranean. The sun cracked shafts of light on the beach below, all fucked up, thick, rich, jewelry light that said lustily "let's get naked and lie really close." The slopes had been cultivated into vineyards terraced by the years of scurried activity, probably people hypnotised by the romantic sex light that was banging away at those hills looking for an heir. The sheer cliffs clutched small beaches between their rocky knees all nervous virgin energy. This was Cinque Terre. You could bring anyone there and they would fall in love with you. Cue travelogue music.

But what a beach – it was all stones that pressed into you with a kind of delicious pain. No sand. The water was saltier than blood and almost as warm. It was the first s/m beach I had ever encountered.

"I want to get a boat and paddle out to this quiet part of the beach so we can fuck." Giacomo made the word fuck sound the way it should, like a thrust.

"I'm not too keen on taking a boat out with my passport in my knapsack."

"Fine. I thought you would like it though." It didn't matter what I thought actually. The boats were not out for rent because of a storm earlier in the day so we couldn't even if I wasn't be pissy. Giacomo was pissed at me for being a bitch about that.

The storm had brought false memories up out of the bottom of the sea. Terracotta tiles and sandals that had been sea-buffed smooth. Glass that looked like pieces of hard candy, all sandblasted into something that would look less impressive at home on my bathroom shelf. I filled my pockets.

Giacomo was doing his 'ignore me' thing that he does to get a rise out of me. I think he loved to see me in distress. It's a subtle revenge for leaving him at the end of the week to his life of this and that and maybe's. He lay on the beach in a bathing suit that was too big and stretch out for him and pretended I wasn't there. Well, only until I got in the water and then he watched me come out soaking wet with the outline of my dick stuck to my leg. Jutting prominently I might add.

At least I know how to get his attention. I think that swimming is a real test, like dancing. When you see someone swim badly it can ruin a romance.

We got the towels down and we lay on the rocks as if they would eat us. The water was shifting from green to blue as the light played upon the trees above us on the hillsides. The air was warm and full of the smell of laurels.

Giacomo's cell phone rang. It was an old Motorola phone.

"I can iron my shirts with this, it's so heavy and gets so hot if I talk too long on it."

It was Ruggero. He was incredulous at the choice of Monterosso.

"He says it is too depressing."

"It's beautiful." I was always defending Giacomo back then. Embarassingly so, like my brother's old girlfriend. ("But I LOVE him.")

"I brought him here because I think he is a poet." He winked to me while he hung up the cell. And perhaps it was poetic when he gave me the handjob there in the parking lot that was just a clearing in the woods by the side of the road. At least it felt like the best poetry I ever wrote.

"I think you like to be loved, but that you don't like to love." He hung up on Ruggero.

The clouds slipped away. The light broke off in shards as it fell behind the mountains. People jammed the umbrellas up higher on the beach. We sat closer to the water.

He was mumbling to me right now, I couldn't figure out what he was saying. He was asleep or pretending to be.

We left late in the day and on the way back to Milano, he stopped the car at a rest area.

"I'm a bit tired. I can't drive when I am like this. Let me rest a second."

Giacomo fell asleep. I sat in the car as if I was on a summer vacation with my family. The sun was gone and the lights from the highway and the tiny rest area shed were yellow. He began to snore. It was weird; here I was watching someone sleep at a rest area in Italy.

After about an hour of this I had to wake him up. I wanted to get going. It was like the last ritual of some weird matrimony. I didn't want to waste any more time in that car thinking. I wanted to shove off. I wanted to shrug off all this romantic bullshit. At least, I kept telling myself that.

When we got back to the flat my skin was salt-tight and sunburn-dry.

He wet the shower curtain so it would stick to the wall to keep the cold air out.

His lips moved along the line of my chin. He pressed his waist against me. We were soapy. The shower was really hot. It was like a safe place. I thought the water would melt us together.

"You are nicest man I have ever met."

And my sad, fucked up mind turned this into an insult. An insult as heart popping as "I don't love you." Even though his "I love you's" did sound like goodbyes.

The bedroom was warm when we got out but that stupid toilet that he hadn't fixed yet--it ran water all night long.

The randomness of the morning was putting me on edge. I preferred to wake up and jump out of bed and get moving but this day I was glued to the mattress. Giacomo had long ago left the bed for work.

Solange had me ticking through a list of special pet peeves that have annoyed me and reminded me of the people screaming at the French restaurant. I didn't actually hear them when it was happening- I guess I stored some of the memories away for later access.

The good news was that the other people who had only gotten sick at Giacomo's restaurant had all been taken off the critical list. The seafood had been ruled the cause and Giacomo had to deal with some super irate patrons who demanded the head of the chef. Prepare for a serious investigation. Death by botulism food poisoning was rare in Italy. Maybe one or two people a year in Lombardia, although most of those would be in Milano. Unfortunately, this year had picked Giacomo's. It would be investigated fully.

The restaurant had to close for a good bit. It would surely reopen later, "under new management." In a couple of months they'd stick a model named Fawn or Shalala from Giacomo's agency at the front door as hostess and no one would think twice.

I don't think the chef had been happy though. They found him dead in a car down the street.

The sky at Malpensa was ripped-out cotton stuffing dragged through an ashtray.

"I am confused."

"How do you feel?"

"I don't know. I am not sure."

"You are 47 years old. You know how you feel." You fucking bastard. An airport's not the place for half-assed emotion. I can turn any goodbye into the last scene in *Casablanca*.

The plane would not take off. It taxied all the way to Berlin. That dream repeats a lot. And I get off the plane, which is going so slow that I can walk alongside it so I can clear away any rabbits or cats or dogs that it might crush. It's like a scene from that bad Star Wars prequel.

I wonder if Solange ever got really scared. I tried to remember what it was like to not fly around Europe like a wannabe jetsetter. I tried to remember what it was like to be in Italy.

I left big chunks of heart in Italy. I think I fell in love with Italy more than Giacomo. He was just available, attractive, wealthy and a half dozen other things that can feel like a prelude to love. He was easy. There are parts of our conversations that float up into my conscious every so often and it always makes me feel like I'd been stolen. I felt like I had all this pinned down but he had ripped it all open and made it sore and broken. Like an egg. There is no way to get it all back together. Need a new one.

I don't know what guides hearts. Maybe it's not even the heart. I thought I knew what it was. I had it all pinned up like a butterfly collection on cardboard- but people don't stay pinned. They want to smack their wings, pull out the pin, stop staining the paper and get off.

I suppose I should be happy I met him and seen the reflection of myself staring back at me. Maybe he was mirror face incarnate.

"Wacky." That's what Kevin would have said.

The plane moved into my plans and tore me away. Italy was something on a map again. The plane ride was uneventful, except I had the distinct feeling that one of the flight attendants used to chat with me online. He kept giving me this cyber kinda vibe. I think his name was Marcel or Marshall, looks French Canadian. Ancient chopping-wood-all-day-long genetics give them that solid look. He had one of those big beefy muscular asses that makes you want to slap it 'til it's red.

At the Hotel Excelsior in Berlin, just a few steps from the forlornly weird outdoor YMCA-pool-like Ernst Reuter Platz, Solange suddenly became talkative.

"Germans are the only ones who like my singing voice. I've been flavor of the month here so many times that I come in regular and diet version."

"Like cherry coke."

Solange loved to say the word 'flavor' like 'flava' but of course if you asked her to write the word down she would spell it 'flavour." Solange's real name was Loretta. I think. I tried to get a look at her passport at the hotel front desk but she was quick.

"Like cherry coke without the cherry." I said from the shower. "False advertising."

The Berlin Excelsior lobby would inspire an impromptu Fassbinder film festival inside anyone's head.

"So don't you love this hotel?"

"It's really seventies. Black leather and mirrors with chrome. It's like a Studio 54 on board the Death Star."

"I love it."

The phone rang.

"That'd be for me." Solange hopped to the phone. The nail polish on her toes was drying. She was heavy on the whispering. And although I desperately wanted to feel desperate and ruthless I simply couldn't muster the feeling that I was 'on the run' with my accomplice. I just felt slightly heartsick.

The phone rang a lot in room 215 at the Excelsior. Solange had a lot of people in Berlin hooking her up with stuff. She said it was video equipment- it was all in her manic German which I couldn't understand, although it sounded production manager-ish to me. We shot a segment at a cute Italian place called Mondo Pazzo. I felt like Solange was trying to remind me at every turn about Italy.

I spent a few days looking the city over. The history here was heavy and bleak. It edges the whole bourgeoisie vibe with a kind of suicide shopping spree feeling. The weather doesn't help. I was ready for some purpose. Or at least a good time.

The second day in Berlin Solange breezed into my room with all these seashells woven into her dready braids. She was really into it for about a week and kept telling everyone that the shells had this meaning and that she had collected them herself. Finally I got sick of it and said really loud.

"Why do you want to look like a rock as the tide goes out?"

"You think? I thought it was kinda cool."

She was pissed at me. But the hairstyle changed a day later. I don't know why I got annoyed. I don't like to make judgments of people. I'm rarely impartial. Maybe it was the tail end of my own realization that she was not some fairy creature, some firefly bestowing immortal coolness to those she touched. She was just an interesting, worldly woman with a (mostly) great dress sense who sporadically poisoned people. And what I didn't know wouldn't kill me, yet.

She complained about bad service in a way that actually worked. Usually I hated when I was with someone who made a big scene but she could pull it off. She freaked about a roach at the Versace store on the Ku-Damm. She was really bitchy, but in a strange way it was mostly directed at the roach. Although she did say: "I will let some people I know in on your roach problem here at this upscale locale- unless I could be hushed up somehow."

The sales associates were running around the register and the display cases trying to smack this big ass roach. Solange put a hand on her hip.

"What do I have to do to get some service in this store? Kill the roach myself??" She started humming "Hedonism" by Skunk Anansie. Maybe the staff thought she was Skin, the lead singer. It worked.

I think she got a pair of pants out of it. It didn't see her pull out a credit card or cash. It pays to bring a big shopping bag to a roach hotel like that.

In the midst of this frenzy I got a SMS on my cell from Giacomo. It just said "She distracted me with you. Love, Giacomo." I saved it but didn't say anything to Solange.

A week later, after removing the Cape Cod National Seashore from her scalp, we went to a party in Mitte. Solange introduced me to a bunch of international exhibitionists and sluts, to be mild. Mitte reminds me of a bunch of cardboard boxes with tissue paper wadded in them. All the presents have been opened- but the boxes are still around.

Most of the people at this party were getting ready for a seasonal migration from Berlin to parts south in Italy. It was a clique of diverse backgrounds. Some rich, some poor, some stupid, some Nobel material. The parties were always at a house that was being renovated slightly or the actual owners were away. A lot of house-sitting and party hopping.

"The best ones were in Italy because the houses and the food were always incredible." Solange loved to open a big fat glossy magazine about Mediterranean life and point to all the dark corners in some villa or casa that she had lurked, having sex or carrying on business.

The migrating party crowd had two things in common, actually three things. Each and every one of them was ridiculously sexy in their own way. They all spoke English without that usual self-conscious foreign-born speaker self-disclaimer "my English is terrible." They knew that it didn't matter. Most had an accent that was an advantage.

They also had the ability to hold one really good conversation. Then most of them were spent. They could rustle up an hour or two of depth. Perhaps the amount of time required to suss out whether they wanted to fuck you, then it was gone – poof. Then it was like trying to talk to a pegboard.

A lot of Italian starlets showed up late.

Solange returned from the bar with drinks for us.

"OK- there she is. I knew she'd be here." She gestured to a busty tanned young woman in a tight vinyl *Matrix*-like dress with long shining perfect hair. Evil hair.

"You knew she'd be here?"

"It's my job to know where these people are."

"Um ok Solange- you're wigging me out here." I thought she was getting jealous or maybe she was hired to do something to this girl. Getting that unsettling feeling.

"She was in the last Dario Argento movie. She had one line- but she didn't get killed which to me was pretty ridiculous. If you are going to be in an Argento movie at least get yourself killed."

Solange wanted to compare horror movie notes with her.

"Ciao Isabella, comé stai?"

"Ciao Solange!" Isabella saw Solange and pushed past two older Italian men to jump up and down vigorously and purposefully in front of them. Her breasts bounced and bumped and barely stayed inside her dress. She took one of the drinks from Solange's hand and slurped loudly and walked over to look in a huge gold framed mirror on the far wall of the room. She seemed to have the i.q. and attention span of a rubber plant.

"Fantastic art collector huh sweetie?" Solange called out to her.

I watched big titty Bella rush up to embrace Solange giggling.

"Yes – it's beautiful but I fear it is only a reproduction." She giggled. Okay, maybe she wasn't a dummy.

"You're too hard on yourself darling, that's my job." Solange smirked but in a pleasant way.

"I loved you in Hypochondria! You are my idol." Isabella effused, jiggling in a Charo kind of way.

"Thank you, grazie." Sometimes Solange would hate it when people brought up her old slasher movie past but sometimes, like tonight- she would love it. If someone really appreciated the stuff she did, she could tell and she was always flattered.

"She had her tits done too early I think." Solange said to me as she moved in closer. "Those must be producers with her, the ones ogling her."

"That's your acting verdict?"

"Um, yeah. No one wants to see a girl with tiny tits killed in an Argento movie. That's why his wife was almost always the final girl- the one that doesn't die. She only got killed off in the daughter's movie."

"I told her that you were a producer too. She should be treating you differently right about now. Expect tits." Solange murmured in my ear as she pulled the empty drink from my hand and replaced it with a new fresh one.

"The hosts and hostesses always had some new place to throw a happening. And the mix of people. They came at you like extras at that party in *Eyes Wide Shut*."

"Italy seems like a hundred lives ago." I was a bit drunk. Solange whirled around to me, like she had remembered she'd left the baby in the car. She beckoned Isabella to meet me.

"Hi there, Solange told me all about you."

"Oh." I couldn't form a thought. Almost all my eyesight was haloed with this silver light- like a slit in my corneas was making the world warp with winter chill. Scribbles of light and color burped around the room.

I'd been dosed.

My mom's fatal party predictions were coming true. My cell phone started ringing. I felt like I was in a rainforest. Everything was shiny and wet looking. My phone vibrated in my hand like a pulse. "I have to take this call, excuse me."

I heard Isabella say something like "He's American?" as I walked into a small bedroom to answer the call.

It was Alain. He had been leaving messages on my voicemail. I was being coy or indifferent, it depended on what he accused me of at the time, but I wanted to see him again.

"John, I miss you and I think about the time in the restaurant and I almost cannot go out to dinner anymore. It's a good thing and a bad thing in one. I don't know what to do."

"I can come to see you. I don't think Solange will be shooting anymore this month." I wish I hadn't used that verb.

"I would love that so much."

"Me too. I think someone dosed me at this party."

A silent (yet very French) pause.

"And you wouldn't come to my dinner- but you go to some weird place with Germans and get drugged? With what?"

"I don't know. Some hallucinogenic. I hope it doesn't last

long."

"Don't go flying out any windows."

"Bye, see you soon."

"Bye John. Be a little more careful."

I felt like someone had Novocained my soul. I walked slowly and deliberately through the coral reef of this bedroom, trying to make back to the main party room. Light from the streetlamps outside made dorsal shapes skit across the walls. I stopped to watch. The drapes flickered the remaining light into pale pathways out into heaven. It was good stuff, whoever put it in my drink was wasting it on me. Then I thought of Cindy disco dumping and blowing apart the restaurant. The reef swayed and trembled. Anonymous chests and bodies disconnected and reformed with pale fronds and swimmer's friction. I was spinning my own head maybe. Trying to find a dull heaven to numb my brain in. Find someplace where I can zone out and never get too close to the burning part of me that continues to live and grasp at time.

I passed through the undersea kingdom and saw Solange swimming in the middle of a clearing of kelp.

"I'm going to Paris." I announced to Solange, stumbling into her and Isabella. "Someone dosed my drink too. I think its really good acid with some E." I ran my hands up and down Solange.

"God that is so 1988, fucking candy-flipping in Berlin. What is this? The fucking love parade?" Solange said that altogether too loudly, looking around the room with dark eyes.

Isabella gave her a sharp look, then put her hands on her hips.

"Are you ok John? Do you want to go back to the hotel and rest. We can go now." Tits tits tits.

"I want to go back to Paris and see Alain."

"Ok, but not this minute right? Because you look a bit nuked. You need to lie down for a bit. Let me get you some water." Solange seemed a bit competitive with Isabella's attention. Boy was I reading that wrong.

"I want to know who did this."

Isabella got weirdly annoyed. She didn't know me and she got so angry, like I was her brother or something.

Solange went to the kitchen to get some water.

Isabella stared around the room with angry doe-eyes. People didn't seem to notice that I was trying to fly-fish, swooping my imaginary rod into their midst. Isabella straightened her tits in her vinyl and then brought my hands firmly down into my lap. She looked over her breasts straight into my slap-happy eyes and said:

"Solange dosed you."

Of all the crimes (and life makeovers) I can accuse Solange of perpetrating I think the most annoying one is that she kept proving me right about all my decisions. I mean, yes, I was probably delusional. She'd only been half a siren, luring me part way to the rocks. I was the one that threw myself down them. When the purpose was so bound to the personality how can you excavate that? I can only be the best of what I have. Of what I've been given and although that doesn't fit into what I had in mind, its me nonetheless. It's all I could ever hope to be. All I had the power to dream.

I wasn't mad at her for dosing me- I mean, how could I really believe Isabella anyway. Who were any of these people really?

I went to the Hotel Excelsior alone without telling Solange I was leaving. I didn't look for her in the crowd. I was hoping to run past her and get a decent amount of space between us so that I think. I couldn't be measured with the ordinary rulers I had around. I wanted to be seen by the way a planet or a star wobbled. I was snorkeling through cabs and lobbies. The drug began to slack but it had been a powerful trip.

Enough to knock me down a bit for awhile. I didn't want to know why.

In the hotel room I took all the money from her secret hiding pockets. I knew where she kept it all. I took her gun, which was still in one of her bags. I didn't know anything about guns but I wanted to stop her from using this one. I had a vision of her now in my head, at a beach, the two of us knee deep in waves, with her gun raised to my head.

I called the train ticket agency and charged it to her card. I had been doing all her business odds and ends so long now it was like I wasn't doing it illegally. I actually didn't think too much about whether it was right or wrong. I just knew that I couldn't fly with all this money and a gun, that they wouldn't search me if I took a train into France. I could avoid all that. Yeah I was paranoid but I also didn't want to get caught with it. I just wanted to be back in Paris, helping Alain with his restaurant aversion therapy and getting away from the She-poisoner of Giallo.

The train ride was almost as fast as I had hoped. It was overnight, straight to Paris from Berlin. I got on at Zoo Station and lay in a bunk above a German couple who desperately needed some vitamin D or whatever gives skin a decent glow. They were mushroom gray. They reminded me of all the aliens that *In Search of* had always theorized about. The Grays. They insisted on shutting off the lights at 6 pm. I didn't want to argue so I let them. I made one phone call to Alain to let him know that I was on my way. I think he was thrilled.

He was waiting at Gare Du Nord. It always felt like a postcard to me there. He had this smile on his face that made me feel like I had reached the proper escape velocity from Solange. She couldn't drag me back to crash.

"Hey there Mr. John." He hugged me and made those motions for my bags that helpful people make.

"I can handle it Al."

"Again with Al, please!" But he was smiling wider. It was so nice to be somewhere with someone who just liked me. Who was waiting for me to speak. A conversation.

"Okay, Alain. I get stuck in a habit. How are you?"

We walked. My luggage wheels made scratchy mental d.j. sounds on the street.

"So how is Solange? How is the project?"

"I think that whole thing is um, on hiatus." I didn't want to talk about anything real. I wanted to fall into Paris and let it fill me up with new everything. I wanted to let go of all my expectations and all the fucked up shit that had happened.

"Oh. Well we'll have a good dinner tonight. I've made some really good stuff recently at home."

"And you haven't left the house much huh?"

He fell silent, pretended to be concerned about oncoming traffic.

"Have you gone out at all recently? Was this your first big trip out?"

Still more silent bashful avoidance.

"We are going to restaurant tonight."

"But I made food."

"You haven't been to a restaurant since we met. You have to break that feeling. You have to get out. Or you'll never."

"Never what? Never get shot? I'm sick of crowds. I am just starting to feel better."

"Good, so we can go to a restaurant."

"Okay."

At the restaurant he was a bit scattered. Looking around and acting like he was thinking of robbing the place even though I knew the exact opposite was true. By the main course he had settled down and was behaving somewhat normally.

"What will you do now? How long will you stay?"

"I don't know. I think I want to rest a bit. I've been trying to keep up with someone who has a really weird hectic lifestyle."

"Yeah, I can only imagine."

"Exactly."

We had coffee and some chocolate cake for dessert.

"See, you lived through dinner."

"Yes I know, thanks."

"It's my job to get people through dinner alive." Or at least that's what it had been.

My cell phone began to play "Get UR Freak On." The phone didn't bother Alain. He was still asleep. The sunlight moved so slowly over his face from the open window as the sun set. As my eyes adjusted to the light his face becomes less vague but he kinda glows. It's a very pretty picture. His body was getting a little soft though- which is totally my fault. My fault and also this all-vegetarian restaurant that he goes to on his lunch breaks. He had the non-dairy whipped cream dessert thing everyday. At least he doesn't snore.

It was Solange.

"I'm in Paris." She was hyper.

"What the fuck?"

For the record she was wearing no bra, a gauzy black top (see-through,) a vintage Gucci belt and new black Versace jeans.

"Baby I am at the hotel and I am scared shitless."

"What? I can't believe you." I wanted to scream at her and get mad- but I also wanted to know what she was scared about.

"You know the guy at Giacomo's restaurant--the orange

one?"

"Yeah, the fake tan guy?"

"He came up to me at a café this afternoon and threatened me."

"He's in Paris?"

"He scared the hell out of me- the orange one."

"Yikes. Oh god."

"I know."

"He threatened you?"

"Baby, that guy's face is a threat. His breath could melt teeth. I told him I was looking into becoming a flight attendant."

"Really" My hair-raised giggles. "Really?"

"Yeah, I know- I thought it was funny too- that's why I said it but then he said that that would be a safer place for me- in the sky"

"Oh I don't like that."

"I know- neither did I. But they didn't follow me."

"So you are at the hotel now?"

"Yes. I have the room for a week- then I guess I start flight attendant school." She laughed a little but I could tell she was scared. Her bracelets tapped on the receiver making a clicking sound–I could hear them on my side, she was waiting for me to talk again. What was I supposed to say?

"I'm at Alain's, but I'll come there. But I want to know why you did it."

"Baby it wasn't meant for you. I don't know- if you don't believe me its my own fault. But if he's here it's because he knows about my part in all that stuff in Milan. Duh."

"I don't care about whether it was for me or not. It has to stop. I have to stop. I feel like my head is about to pop.

"I didn't have anyone I could trust. I'm sorry."

"They don't know where you are staying- it won't be a problem. His place is a bit of a ways from the hotel too- we can meet halfway and talk."

"Ok, I guess that sounds good. Of course I want to see you and I hate this weather and being alone."

"Don't open the door for any strangers."

"Yeah I was thinking of that.'

"Let's meet by the bridge that you like. We can talk about all the shit that's going down."

"OK. Give me about twenty minutes."

"Ciao."

"Ciao."

I was going to tell her that I had taken her gun but I figured she already knew. It didn't matter anyway. I was later than twenty minutes.

From across the street I could see her arguing with three men. She was wearing a blue shawl. It reminded me of what Nona Hendryx would wear twenty years ago. The cars between us made a peek-a-boo game of the tension. I almost shouted to her but some force inside me had clamped my mouth shut. Some evil part of me was playing spectator again. Like an out of body experience.

A small red car flew past and the orange man was revealed pressing his dirty orange finger into Solange's face. My brain was processing all this data before me, trying to break it down to a conclusion I should have reached on the phone with her. All that came up was Giacomo's face. The traffic whooshed.

The argument seemed to be over. Solange walked a few steps away. But then, with all the casualness of a bunch of lethargic house cats, they took hold of her, lifted her over the bridge's railings and let her go. It happened so fast that it seemed mundane. Someone doing a chore. It happened so fast that I didn't cry out or move. And Solange did not struggle. She went regal- her whole face and body, like they were hoisting her onto a horse or a throne. Obviously something had tipped

Giacomo off. I don't think it was me. He had gone out of his way to let certain people know. He'd betrayed Solange. Probably with good reason of course but he'd betrayed me. Now I was convinced I had changed. It scared me to think that I may become really old and never get free of this dirty feeling, the feeling that people who don't feel guilty never have.

In two seconds I realized that not only was I a terrible human being but that I had about three *more* seconds to live if they caught me staring in their direction. I didn't run. I didn't look at anything but the gray sidewalk. Sweat ran down the backs of my legs. My arms felt limp and weak. I had a horrible ringing in my ears. The sound of Solange hitting the water cleared it. That and the sight of the waiter Solange had fucked at Giacomo's restaurant crossing to my side of the street.

My head filled up with electricity, he seemed to be shooting it at me with his eyes. I thought my own eyes would pop out. I thought that I would liquefy, run down the sides of my shoes as my clothes collapsed onto themselves.

All around me voices. Many voices that were saying things in beautiful words. Words that I could barely understand literally but I could understand the emotion. People were beginning to react to what had happened. What they had thought they had seen or heard. The thugs were already gone. Only the waiter seemed charged with cleaning me up.

I couldn't speak. Somewhere a long time ago when language was born, when a grunt of pain or pleasure passed into syllables and became a commonality. The differentiation of an object from an emotion. A verb from a noun, this was a new kind of language. They had never needed a tense before. Everything was now. Everything was. There were no yesterdays. No tomorrows. Words for vomit, revulsion and disease. All words that rose out and stretched among the puddles of blood. Removing themselves from emotion. Distancing the reality of reaction. Falling, to the water- a broken neck. Solange was dead but her voice was in my head.

Now I had to begin the real work that had been bequeathed to me all along. And I admit, I was crazy at this point. I had no idea what I really should have done.

I couldn't be a successful killer like Solange if I didn't feel guilty. Guilt was a No-Doze. It would keep me aware of the risk and the need for caution. If I didn't allow for and feel the depth of the crime then how could I hope to understand the need to avoid the severity of the punishment? And if that waiter was coming for me I would take him down. With every bit of whatever was in me. I would kill him. I would get away.

I would punish Giacomo.

Everything in me rebelled against the ideas forming in me about Kevin and Solange. They flew around like birds in my head.

I felt alive now. Awake. Pumped with adrenaline and sweat and fear and loathing. The sun came down on me like hot/cold metal. Everything was lethargic, razor sharp and unyielding but as commonplace as a heartbeat.

I had a way. No matter what Solange had done, she

didn't deserve to be thrown off a bridge. I just had to get past this one waiter.

But I was wrong. He didn't recognize me. He just walked past me, confident, indifferent, ignorant- like a tourist.

My lightweight black Tumi bag was stained. I'd been nervous and split a coffee on it. But that had cleared my head and steadied my nerves. Earlier, getting off the train at Milan Centrale Station it had been the lightest luggage I had ever carried--but I had acquired Solange's most potent fashion accessories on my way to Giacomo's.

I got a room at a cheesy new business class hotel near Via Conca Del Naviglio and went through the Internet, researching. In the bathroom I cleaned Solange's gun, double-checking with an informative website I'd found. Slowly, the gun took shape, like a butch clarinet. I was now convinced that this gun was the gun that no one would ever find lying at the bottom of the Atlantic. This gun or a gun just like it might have killed Kevin, albeit- with his blessings. Now Solange's adoption and sponsorship of me made sense in ways that I didn't want to understand, but I couldn't escape. I was held in place, on pause. My violence was skittering on the top of it all, like a water strider on a Dracut pond when I was nine years old. Feelers and antennas searching out the next event to bloom.

Across the street, through the window I could see BABY

JESUS IS A CHAMP spray-painted in Italian across the underpass.

When I was halfway satisfied that I knew how to load and use the gun I put it in the bag and left the hotel.

Viale Tibaldi is divided in the middle by a tramway. The bus goes down the middle of it. It's like a large ashtray someone had planted some weeds in. The fish market nearby never smelled fresh. It was a low tide in the hot sun--reminds me of 10 year old me, lying on Daytona Beach, listening to the Pet Shop Boys' *Please* cassette tape with a Walkman I bought at Sears. I ate ice cream everyday and got so tan my mother didn't recognize me when she saw me at the end of the summer. The Italian sun here is like that too- the mother of that sun.

The apartment building had a courtyard hidden by a big door from the street. In the big door was a tiny door that can be buzzed. It was standard for this part of the city. I had banged my head hard on this little door a few months ago, drunk. The little door would be locked so I had to go around to the other side. Here was where I could watch and wait. If he had not gone to work on time (he is always late) he would be watering the plants right about now.

I bought a dumb magazine at the station to read. The article about people's body language was a real scream. I scanned through it to see if any of 'her' heterosexual body language could be superimposed onto a more gender-neutral situation.

Giacomo's head bobbed in the frame of the window. He

looked like an elf in the morning sunlight. Towards the middle of the afternoon he'd begin to resemble someone you could fall in love with, if he would just keep his mouth shut for five minutes.

He snapped the screen up. The screen was a floor to ceiling screen that I had always had a hard time getting to stay down. He was a pro at it. He didn't look like someone that would have someone killed. He looked like the guy I had fallen in love with and felt like a little kid with. Somehow, maybe he hadn't been responsible for Solange. But he had been responsible for my heart. All I could feel was my "pawnhood." That they had moved me around in whatever way seemed opportune for their own spoiled decadent designs. Maybe he thought I was in on it. Who knows?

Killing him would be a kind of suicide. I didn't have a handle on that yet and what it meant to me. I didn't have a clue except that it was my usual self-centered response to violence, whether or not I was the one responsible for it or not. I just wanted to have an effect on my environment that was in my control. Admitting that now makes me realize how whack I was. Nothing I did now would make much of a difference to Solange regardless. Still I was compelled. The abrupt jerk of Solange over the railing of the bridge compelled me.

The one bullet would pop his head like a zit. Only one. So quiet- it could be confused with a bird shitting on his balcony. He'd make a low thud and the watering can would pitch over end to the courtyard. It would end up watering the weeds that were growing around a flowerpot I had stared at in the mornings of a few lifetimes ago

But I didn't do it. I just didn't care about anything anymore. I didn't care about him- that may have stopped me. He finished watering the plants and I watched him until he disappeared into the apartment. Later, on the street, I watched him desperately try to remember where he had parked his car. I don't know if he saw me. It doesn't really matter. I hadn't done anything wrong. Sorry, let me restate that- I hadn't done anything illegal. I threw the bag with Solange's gun into a bush by the side of the trash bins. I imagined it fossilized there, the bubbles from its barrel were just silicone snail trails now.

Solange. She'd probably dragged me around Europe to cover herself anyway. I hadn't wanted to believe that but why not? It was just as easy to believe her wanting me around just to talk to. With me there, haunting all the same places that she had- it would be easy to pin some of her crazy schemes and stratagems on me. I would be the Wilma in her wacky retelling of *The Maltese Falcon*. I'd been involved with that idiot Giacomo. I'd had ample opportunity to fuck around with the kitchen at the restaurant. Not to mention the fact that she had almost always insisted we travel separately. Tax write-offs or clever ploys. I don't know if it even matters now. Although her constant insistence that we travel separately had spared me any entanglement in her murder investigation. No one could trace me to her. Everything had been cash. I was invisible. In a different box.

Bitterness that I couldn't allow to flavor me was swelling

up. I had to beat all that down into submission. All that cynicism was dead wood. It couldn't possibly fuel a career let alone a lifestyle. Even if Giacomo wanted to, he wouldn't be able to reach me in the usual way. I had the numbers changed. Got myself a new email account.

He could try rubbing lamps, rubbing rings. Try all the ways he spun my hopes into the blue, blue sky. I'd be rooting for him. Wherever I am. Maybe someday we could talk about it. Maybe then he wouldn't think of me as that special time in the summer of yadda yadda year. I'll just be a guy he knew for a short time that suddenly disappeared. And he'll be weary to talk with me but might do it anyway. And I will thank him in the only way I know how. Fancy that?

Maybe then I can convince myself that I was really trying to do something important. I was trying to prove a point. But then again that could be misinterpreted and we would fall silent, watching the sun set and softly begin counting the first sprawl of stars kneeling into the sky.

I walked away. I walked a long distance away and then I put a plane ride between him and me.

In Boston the summer had forgotten what it was supposed to do. Cold rainy days are great for clearing my head. Or they match my frame of mind so that I feel like a camouflage has been thrown down on me. There was no sound from the street today- everyone has given up doing anything in the weather. I took a shower in the hotel and it was like a perfect scene in a movie. The soap lathered into crazy thick sheets and the warm water gushed all over me. It was soothing. I slipped into bed.

My memories of him are now clouded. In time perhaps he'll be a simple tiny event, after all, what is 6 months in someone's life?

I felt like someone abducted by a u.f.o. and then returned. The aliens of course had gotten me addicted to slow heartbreak or maybe the implant is faulty. Felt good going in.

I went to my parents house on the Cape. I wanted to go to Normal, USA and try to reset my brain. Days passed there like dull gray waves of snow.

I got an astrologically well-timed call from Alain. He had flown to Boston on a whim- he's one of those guys that works all the time, has two jobs and money from his parents and can just fly around whenever he feels like it. Anyway, he missed me and wanted to see me again. It was a good dose of normal emotion for me.

We went to a bar danced slowly in the back of the room. It was dark and I was just drunk enough to be able to read body language flawlessly.

 The music wrapped around us- it was that kind of sleazy venue that I never get too into and don't immerse myself in too often- but a lot of guys turn it into a kind of weekend retreat. Alain was wearing these really old jeans that had holes in the backside. After I had made a few more holes in the backside of his jeans trying to get them off him I realized he was wearing a jock under them. I don't know what you call our relationship. I told him all about Solange and the botulism toxin. Midway through I realized that I was using him as my father confessor. Just like Solange. Maybe she'd rubbed off on me.

We went to Cape Cod that weekend to spend some time on the beach. He kept talking about Francois Ozon's *Under the Sand* and that lent a macabre vibe to the whole thing but it was warm and mellow. Sand was pressing against my legs. In that bathing suit I got in Paris with Solange. I could feel the heat again. All the beats.

Kevin was slowly receding into my personal history. History that folds a person's life into a parcel that maybe no one will remember to claim. He's already time traveling. In a few years I will be older than him. Spooky to think that. If I become an old man leaning out over the sea on some terrace somewhere, he will be young and shining in pictures forever. He never let age touch him.

I forced myself to see Monterosso again. The beach was grabbing onto the mountains there. Clutching at them and filling the holes under the arches that hold up the trains. I wanted to ride those trains again. I even wanted to see Giacomo smile again.

It was a moment in time that made me realize everything in my life, no matter how far in my past; everything in my life is connected, strung together by minutes. It's a continuous thrust forward and though I may try and cordon off bits and pieces of it with stupid names like adolescence or twenty-something- it all flows forward without any stopgaps. It is not going to stop until it actually does.

That might have made me shiver a bit, but West Dennis Beach was hot, hazy and well lit like a Rothko should be. Nothing moved except the waves and even they seem reluctant to touch the beach. Delicate avoidance. Almost enough to call disdain. We had walked to the end of the beach, setting the towels down on the place where I have always gone since I was 15. My place to get a handle on what was breaking me into little self-pity parts.

I watched Alain bake in the sun. I wanted him to really care about me- like I wanted to care about him. I wanted him to think of me when I wasn't around. Not the way I think of Solange. Not the way I remember Kevin, not in those subtle memories that bob up when someone smells a certain way. I want it all. I want him to feel an echo of me in each beat of his heart. I want to infect him with a bit of my obsession. Then I'll know I can live forever. I guess all that kind of crazy romantic stuff takes time. I promised myself to slow down.

The sky was blue, empty and quiet- just the voice of the ocean repeating into it. It only said one thing, but did so perfectly, over and over.

Alain shielded his eyes with his hand and looked up at me. The beach behind him framed his face like a portrait. He stared at me silently, smiling.